PREY & PRAY

JUDI GUAY

Acknowledgments

I would like to thank my husband Gary, my family, and my friends for their immeasurable support and belief in me while I was writing this book. I'd also like to thank my computer guru Bob for his expertise. In addition, I would like to give special heartfelt thanks to Judy (Eastman) Jackson for using her knowledge, talent, and patience while editing my book.

Dedication

To my brother, Austin Miller, with love and gratitude for your support, and to my dear friend Kayla Kemp.

Table of Contents

Table of Contents

Chapter One - The Abduction

As daylight fades away and darkness moves in, I feel compelled to satisfy my strong sexual needs. Overpowering the minds of helpless women with utter fear and performing sexual acts on them against their will has always been my foremost obsession. My deep hunger for both causes me to seek them out, wait, and then prey on these unsuspecting women, as if I were a wild animal hunting down my next meal. Once again, I will do whatever I have to do to satisfy my needs. I am, at this very moment, in search of my next victim.

I'm driving on a narrow graveled country road searching for a honky-tonk bar called the Five Mile Roundup. It was advertised on several different billboards next to the interstate that I have been traveling on. Where there's a bar, there are usually women. It's located in a very remote area away from the city and all of those damn arrogant cops.

It looks like I have reached my goal. I'm approaching the building now; I can hear loud country music coming from inside. I'm going to pull into the field up ahead and drive behind that dense area of tall trees and heavy brush to park.

I have covered a lot of miles in the last couple of days, and the muscles in my arms and legs are very sore. I need to get out of this truck and stretch so I can get some blood circulating through my body again and check out the area.

After reaching into the back of the truck to get what is needed to help abduct my next victim, I am walking toward the club. As I push the tall weeds aside I can see a young woman through the tree branches who has just parked her car at the edge of the lot. She is opening her car door and swinging her feet out to step on the ground. Her dress is hiked up above her thighs, and her shapely bare legs are slightly parted as she begins to stand up. She is straightening her dress and throwing the strap of her purse over her shoulder as she starts to walk alone across the dark area toward the club. Just the thought of mounting and penetrating that little filly like a stallion is causing me to get an erection.

I am completely out of everyone's sight, hiding behind a large tree right next to her car. Crouched down with my limbs bent like a spider, I will be able to quickly lurch toward her from behind when the time is just right.

The parking lot is very crowded with cars and is dimly lit. It is starting to lightning and thunder, and small patches of fog are lingering in the air above the ground. I have a large piece of netting draped over my shoulder, and while I'm waiting for her to return to her car, I'm preparing a syringe and needle with a strong tranquilizing drug. I am beginning to feel drops of rain hitting against my bare chest and the mask that is covering my face.

After an hour of waiting and watching for her to return, I am becoming very impatient. My heartbeat is increasing rapidly, my breathing feels labored, and I am finding it very difficult to contain my eagerness to seize what will soon be mine. It is then that I will strip her of all her dignity and strength by taking complete control of her mind and body.

I can see her exiting the door of the club now, and as she is walking across the lot, there is a slight breeze causing her dress to flow against her bare legs and reveal the shape of her body. Her mind seems to be very preoccupied as she is messaging someone on her cell phone. With no one else in the lot right now, apprehending her will be a much easier task than I thought.

She is getting closer and closer to her car. As I watch her walk in those high heeled shoes, I can see her hips shifting gracefully from side to side, definitely causing my sexual desires to become much stronger.

She is now walking around the back of her car and turning toward the driver's side; she is only about an arm's length away from me. Her back is toward me as she reaches for the door handle. I jump up and leap toward her to grab her by her hair, and as I pull her head back, I jab the needle deep into her neck. I quickly swipe the netting over her head and shoulders tightly to secure her. She is now trapped like a small insect in a large web, totally helpless and entangled.

As I struggle to pull her through the wet, tall weeds to my truck, I feel a very masculine sense of power and a deep throbbing sensation in my groin. She is starting to show signs of weakness from the drug as I drag her up the ramp into the back of my truck, but I know that when I pull the door closed behind us, I will have to put aside my strong sexual urge and work very quickly to restrain her.

I am forcing her body down onto the bed that is bolted to the floor of the truck and anxiously tearing off her dress and stripping off her black lacy bra and panties. Now I can spread her arms and legs wide apart and strap them to each corner of the bed. As I look at her flawless bare skin, the bright colored nail polish on her toes, and her luscious naked body, it makes me desperately want to have sex with her now, but I know that I have to leave this place as soon as possible and not take the chance of being seen.

I am taking a picture of her naked body with her cell phone and dumping everything out of her purse. After quickly rummaging through it, I will only keep her address book and driver's license; the rest can be thrown back into her purse. I'm going to hurry back to her car and pitch her cell phone and purse onto the front seat of her car and put the keys back into the ignition.

Feeling slightly out of breath from running back through the weeds and dripping wet from the rain, I have returned to the truck and started it up. After circling back around, I will only have a few miles to drive before I can catch the next exit to the interstate. I can then relax and start fantasizing about the stops that we will be making before we reach our destination.

Chapter Two - The Awakening

I am fighting very hard to keep my eyes open. My body feels cold and clammy, and I am trembling all over. Terrifying images continue to drift in and out of my mind, causing me to feel like I am completely paralyzed in a state of fear. I remember feeling a sharp pain in my neck and the inability to catch my breath from the netting tightly surrounding my face, but the rest I'm struggling to remember.

It is completely dark in here, but I can feel that I have been stripped naked and strapped to a bed, exposing every part of my body. Visions of the perpetrator's evil mask have been deeply embedded into my mind. Please, dear God, help me!

I can hear faint, mournful sounds of either sorrow or pain, and someone is gasping for air. Oh my God, I'm not alone! There is someone in this dark space with me! "God, please hear my prayers. I know that I am going to have to fight for my life. Please watch over me and protect me from the beast that did this to me."

"Radio Check – I know you can hear me on the speaker, Shelby. We have traveled a lot of miles while you were resting. Are you comfortable in that bed? Your driver's license states that your name is Shelby Grey from good old Music City, Tennessee. It says that you are five foot two inches tall, blonde hair, blue eyes, and just turned twenty-six years old.

"Let's get a little light back there for you. Ah yes, now I can see you on the computer screen that is mounted to the dash of my truck. The thought of you being just a few feet away makes it very difficult for me not to pull this truck off the interstate to a quiet place to satisfy my needs. Seeing your naked body strapped to the bed in that position is causing my penis to become hard.

"Turn your head and look to your right; you should feel relieved to know that you are not traveling alone. Say hello to Maggie Lewis. She is still hanging onto life by a thread. I picked her up several months ago in the Windy City in Illinois. I had some good times with her, but she has proven to be a very weak person.

"You can continue to cry and scream, but it will do you no good. I have designed this truck with computers, lighting, and very high-tech equipment, as well as making sure that it is soundproof. You need to save your energy for me, Shelby; you are going to need it. Lights out – you copy me?"

"Oh, God, Maggie, he did say Maggie right? Can you hear me? Please try to concentrate on your breathing; take deep breaths in and out, and try very hard to hang on to the life that God has given you. Please don't give up; we need to fight this beast together. I will pray for us both."

Maggie's hands appear to be tied behind her back, and her skin is very pale. He has placed her in a sitting position on the floor of the truck, and she is slouched over with her head resting on her chest. Her naked body is surrounded by a pool of blood, and she is very thin and dirty. "Please dear God, I don't know what else to do but pray. She is in a lot of pain. Please help her, and don't let her die. Show me what I can do to escape from this beast so that I can help Maggie, and please give us the strength that we are both going to need to survive."

I must have fallen asleep again, or slid into an unconscious state of mind, but I can once again feel movement around me and the vibration of the tires pounding on the pavement.

"Radio check – I will be pulling this truck off the interstate soon."

"Mister, can you hear me? I am in a lot of pain. I really need to go to the bathroom when you stop. Can you hear me?"

"There is a small town up the road off the interstate. I want to pick up a local newspaper and grab a bite to eat, and I need to decide what to do with Maggie."

"Mister, please listen to me. What are you going to do to Maggie? Haven't you already hurt her enough?"

"Radio check – I can hear and see you Shelby. Trust me, Maggie should be the least of your worries, but she could become a problem if she dies back there. In this heat her body would decompose very quickly, and the stench would be overwhelming. And Shelby, don't wet the bed; you can hold it awhile longer. Over and out."

"God, I know that we should never question the plan that you have for our lives and that we should always know that you are watching over us, but why is this happening to us, and how many other women has he done this to?"

The movement of the truck has stopped and I can feel the vibration as the cab door opens and shuts. I can only lie here feeling completely helpless and wondering what he is going to do to us next. My body is shaking all over, and it is dark and quiet in here except for the faint whimpering sounds coming from Maggie and the sound of my own heart beating in my chest. The waiting and the unknown are unbearable. Where can he be, and what is he doing? At least an hour has gone by since he stopped this truck.

I don't think I have ever felt this much fear. Why did I go to that bar? My friend would have understood if I had declined her invitation. I have always had a fear of the dark, so why didn't I have somebody walk me to my car? Please God, spare Maggie from any more pain.

I feel the cab door opening and shutting again, and the truck is starting to move. Approximately half an hour has passed by, I think, and it's starting to feel like the truck is beginning to sway back and forth. He must be driving on a rougher road. Every bump he hits makes me feel like I am going to wet myself.

The movement around me has stopped, and he has turned a dim light back on. The door of the truck is opening and closing again. I can hear him opening the large doors next to me now, and he is pulling down a ramp. With the light from the full moon, I can see the outline of the upper half of his body. I feel like my heart is going to beat out of my chest!

He is beginning to walk up the ramp toward me; he is a tall and muscular man. I am now face to face with a very sick demon. Through the mask he wears, I can see his eyes staring down at my body, and he is turning to glance over at Maggie. The muscles in his arms are twitching and his hands, covered with white surgical gloves, are as steady as a rock.

"Shelby, I am going to lift up your midsection and place this pan under you. Hold nice and still while I insert this catheter in you. I want the pleasure of watching you empty your bladder. There now, that has to feel better doesn't it? I am going to remove the catheter and pull the pan out from under you. Now I can wipe you with this rag. Ah yes, this is so nice. I love looking at you and feeling you down here."

I can see him pulling a knife from a holder on his belt and running his fingers lightly down the blade. He is standing quietly above me, staring at my naked body. "Please dear God, I have never felt so alone. Are you hearing my prayers?"

"Shelby, it is close to 2:00 a.m., and we are in the middle of a small country cemetery just off a gravel road on the edge of Indiana. I drove the last eighth of a mile with the headlights off so that I would be safe from being seen by anybody.

"The eerie feeling of spirits lingering above the graves is so intense, that it actually makes my blood feel as frigid as ice as it flows through my veins.

"I am going to be removing the straps that are restraining your wrists and ankles, and if you try to get away from me, I will make sure that you suffer more than you could ever imagine. Next I will cut the rope off of Maggie's wrists, and I need you to help me get her wrapped tightly in this netting."

"Mister, she is still alive; you are not thinking about burying her are you?"

"No, I'm not going to bury her; you are. Her mind is still aware of what is happening around her, but her body is worn out."

As we are wrapping Maggie's body in the netting, the fear in her eyes is like nothing I have ever seen before. I don't know how I can stop this unmerciful act from happening. The dark bruises on her inner thighs and the open cuts on her body that are bleeding and weeping are marks of the beast. Her heart is still beating. How could this animal do this to her?

"I will grab the shovel hanging on the wall of the truck and help you carry her. I'll lift her feet. You get up by her head and lift, and we will start carrying her down the ramp. Once we get her to the ground, you can just drag her body through the grass between the tombstones."

"Please God, hear my prayers. I don't know what to do to stop this from happening."

"According to the local newspaper I picked up earlier tonight, there was a man by the name of Jason Pratt buried here today. The dirt should be loose enough for you to be able to dig a shallow grave. I can't imagine that Jason would mind having a woman buried on top of him.

"His grave is just up ahead. Stop here for a few minutes, and take a deep breath. If you look closely you can actually see images hovering over the graves. Can you feel all of them watching us? I'm sure they could become very aggressive if they were to get angry.

"Start dragging her again, Shelby. We are almost there.

"Well, it looks like this is where Jason's body has been planted. Alright, start taking all of the flowers off his grave, and set them off to the side. Then you can start digging."

"Mister, please don't do this to Maggie. Her eyes are still open, and she is moaning in pain. I will do anything you ask of me, but please don't do this to her."

"Trust me, Shelby; I am going to do whatever I want to you. Start using that shovel; I am going to start video recording while I just sit here and enjoy looking at your naked body while you dig. You have nice firm breasts and a nice ass; I am looking forward to all of the sex that we will be having when we make our next stop. Maybe, if you can keep me satisfied, I will keep you around for awhile."

"Mister, I need something to drink. I am sweating, and I'm so thirsty."

"Turn around and grab that vase of fresh flowers behind you. Lift the flowers out and drink the water that is left in the vase. Now quit bitching and keep digging.

"Can you feel the spirits gathering around us to watch? It is so powerful it makes the hair on the back of my neck stand straight out. This is a very old cemetery; you can tell by looking at the tombstones. Some are badly chipped and others broken. Rest in peace? That's a joke; there's no chance of any peace here with all this spirit activity going on.

"I think you have dug deep enough. Let's lift her body out of the netting and drop her in the hole. I can reuse this netting."

Maggie's body is still warm. Oh God, what am I going to do? I just noticed that some of her fingertips are missing; this must have been where the pool of blood that she was sitting in came from. If I wasn't feeling so weak, I would try to hit him with this shovel. I am afraid he was right; I can sense someone or something staring at us. I have never in my life felt this terrified.

"Shelby, sit down on the ground next to the hole that Maggie's body is in. I want to capture the two of you together in this recording to send to your mother. Here, hold this bunch of fake purple violets. I will keep some for myself as a memento, and you can drop the rest of them

15

on top of her. Look up at the recorder now; that's good! Now stand up and say your heartfelt goodbye to Maggie, and start filling in the grave."

As I throw the first shovel of dirt on top of her, I can see the horrified look on her face and the tears filling up in her eyes as she looks up at me. "Please, please, dear God and Maggie, forgive me. I am so sorry for being such a weak and selfish person; I am just trying to stay alive."

"Stop sobbing and crying. You will ruin my video. Trust me, she is only going to be gone for awhile, and then she will be back to haunt us both. I am sure of it! Place the flowers back on the grave now, and we will start walking back to the truck."

As we begin to walk, he grabs my arm and wants me to stop. He bends over and picks up a stem of flowers from a grave and asks me to place it between my teeth like a dancer. He tells me to mount a tombstone and indecently pose so that he can once again record it. I am feeling so ashamed and sick.

"Alright, get down from there now, and keep walking!"

After we reach the truck and walk up the ramp, he tells me to lie down and spread my arms and legs wide open, so he can strap me back up to the bed. He then reaches down and slowly starts feeling every inch of my body and inserts his fingers up inside me. The thought of this demented monster touching me, makes me feel like I am going to vomit. I feel so ashamed and dirty.

He is pushing up the ramp now and closing the truck doors. I am mentally, physically, and emotionally drained.

"Dear God, please hear my prayers. I just buried a woman while she was still alive. I didn't even know her. Was she married? Did she have children? What other tortuous acts did he put her through during the last couple of months? She was dropped in a shallow hole in the ground as if her life didn't matter. I feel in my mind and heart that all of the things that my parents taught me about being a good Christian have all been shattered. I have allowed a man to mentally manipulate me into becoming a cold- blooded killer. I am the one that suffocated her with the dirt that I threw on top of her face. God, I am asking you now for your forgiveness."

I can feel the movement of the truck again. We are leaving the cemetery.

Chapter Three - The Quest for Help

"Hi, you have reached the voicemail of Ann Parker. I can't come to the phone right now, so please leave a message, and I will get back to you as soon as I can."

"Ann, this is Peggy, Shelby's mom. It is 9:45 a.m., and I am worried about Shelby. She called me last night and said she was on her way to the Five Mile Roundup to meet you, and that she would call me back by this morning and hasn't. We were supposed to meet for lunch today. I have tried to call her on her cell phone three times, and she's not answering. Please call me when you get this message."

As I roll over in bed and open one eye, I look at the clock and think, "Oh my God; it is almost 10:30 a.m. I must have been very tired to have slept this long. I need to get up and make a strong pot of coffee and take a couple of aspirins to get rid of this pounding headache. I should have left the party last night when Shelby did instead of closing the place up."

While the coffee is running through, I'm going to grab my cell phone and check up on Shelby to see if she enjoyed her party. Huh, it looks like I have a voice message from Peggy. I better call her right back; she sounds very upset.

"Hello."

"Hi, Peggy, this is Ann."

"Oh, Ann, thank you for calling me back. I still have not heard from Shelby, and she is still not answering her phone. Have you heard anything from her since last night?"

"No, Peggy, I was just getting ready to call her when I saw that I had a message from you. I just got up; maybe Shelby slept in, too. Do you want me to drive over to her apartment to check on her since you live an hour away?"

"Could you, Ann? I am worried; this is just not like Shelby."

"I'd be glad to; I will throw some clothes on and drive over right away. I'll call you once I get there. Try to stay calm; I'm sure everything is O.K."

"Thanks Ann, I appreciate it. I will wait to hear from you."

I'm dressed, so I need to grab my coffee, keys, and some aspirin and head over to Shelby's. Peggy is right, this is not like her.

"Hello."

"Hi, Peggy, I'm at Shelby's apartment, but she is not answering her door. I am going to take the elevator down to the parking ramp to see if her car is there. Hang on for just a few minutes. Peggy, her car is not here. Why don't you call the local towing companies to see if she might have had car trouble? I am going to drive out to the Five Mile Roundup to see if her car is sitting along side of the road or in the club parking lot."

"Oh God, Ann, I just don't have a good feeling about this."

"I know, Peggy, but hang in there. Let's not assume the worst. Let's just make sure that we keep in close touch with each other."

My heart goes out to Peggy. She is so worried. She lost her husband, Shelby's Dad, in a car accident a year ago, and Shelby is her only child. I can only say a prayer that everything is going to be all right. She is such a responsible person and so considerate to others; there has to be a good reason why Shelby has not called either one of us.

"Hello."

"Ann, I have called all of the local towing companies and hospitals. She has not been hospitalized, and the towing companies have not received any calls from that area. Should I call the police?"

"No, don't call the police yet. I am only about half a mile from the club. Let me see if her car is there first. I know how upset you are, but no news is good news. I will call you back as soon as I can. Love you!"

I am close to making the second right onto the road to the club. Please dear God, let everything be all right.

I have just reached the entrance to the parking lot. It looks completely empty. Wait - there is a car way over there parked next to the trees. As I am getting closer, I can see that it is Shelby's car. I am going to pull up next to it and check it out. The door is standing open on the driver's side, her keys are in the ignition, and her purse and cell phone are lying on the driver's seat. I need to call the police; something is definitely wrong!

"911, what is your emergency?"

"I need a police officer to come to the Five Mile Roundup club."

"Can I have your name please?"

"Ann Parker, my name is Ann Parker."

"Miss Parker, please calm down. Do I need to dispatch an ambulance or fire truck?"

"No, just please get an officer here right away!"

"Miss Parker, you need to tell me what your emergency is."

"My friend has been missing since last night. Her car is here, but she is not in the car. The car door is open and her purse and cell phone are lying on the seat."

"Miss Parker, do not touch anything. Because the club is located outside of the city limits, I have dispatched a deputy from the County Sheriff's Department, and he should be arriving there soon."

As I stand next to Shelby's car, my mind is racing in a million directions. If something has happened to her, I will never forgive myself for not walking her to her car last night. I feel like this nightmare is entirely my fault.

The county car is pulling into the lot now. I can't stop crying.

"Miss, I am Deputy Ron Taylor from the County Sheriff's Department. What is your name, and can you tell me why I have been dispatched?"

"Sir, I am Ann Parker, and this car belongs to my best friend, Shelby Grey. I had a birthday party for her last night at this club. Her mom and I have not been able to reach her on her phone today. I went to her apartment and she wasn't there, so I drove out to see if her car was here. Her car door was standing open, and her purse and cell phone were lying on the seat."

"Miss Parker, can I please have your driver's license? I would like you to go back to your car and wait for me. I am going to radio the county office and ask for assistance."

"Hi, Peggy, I am at the club and Shelby's car is here. I called 911, and there is a deputy from the Sheriff's Department here now. He has walked over to his county car and is speaking to someone on his radio. Please don't cry. We both need to stay as strong as we can. Peggy, he is walking back toward my car. I will have to call you back."

"Miss Parker, here is your driver's license back, and here is one of my cards. I will need your phone number as well as Shelby's parents' number; the Sheriff's office will be calling you and her parents to come into the department to answer some questions so we can file a report."

"Sir, here, I have already written Shelby's mother's number and my number down for you. Shelby's father is deceased."

"Thank you, Miss Parker. We will get in touch with you both."

As I return to my car, I reach for my cell to call Peggy.

"Hello."

"Peggy, it's Ann. I am on my way back to town. The deputy said that they will be calling us to come into the department to give them some information that they will need to file a report. I think you should come to my apartment and stay with me until we hear something from them."

"Ann, I am so upset right now I can't even think straight. I will pack a bag and be there in about an hour and a half. Please say a prayer for my Shelby. "

Chapter Four - The Chase

"Radio check – it is dark and raining outside. Can you hear the thunder and lightning through the speaker, Miss Shelby? This weather is creating a perfect setting for our last stop before reaching our destination. I have waited a long time for my sexual desires to be satisfied. While you have been in a deep sleep, I have driven almost thirteen hours, not counting the stops I made to refuel the truck. I have given a lot of thought about what games I could play with your mind and body. My so-called mother played some of these same games with me."

"Mister, my mom has probably gone to the police by now. They will be looking for us."

"The police have been searching for many of my victims for years. I don't exist in their system. I was born on a dirt floor of a root cellar surrounded by timber.   I was kept chained up there like an animal for years, so when you call me Mister it seems quite appropriate. You see, I was never given a name."

After lying so long in this position, I am in extreme pain, and I feel very weak from not eating or drinking. I can't get Maggie out of my mind. Every time I close my eyes, I see her looking up at me as I was throwing the dirt on top of her. The guilt that I feel and the fear that is building up in me from knowing what he wants to do to my body are making me horrified and sick.

"God, can you still hear my prayers? I am reaching out to you. I had so many plans for my life, and now I realize that I probably won't have a chance to fulfill any of them. I don't see any signs from you of how I can escape from him. Please don't leave me to fight this beast by myself."

I can feel a definite change in the road and can hear gravel hitting against the underside of the truck. We are now bouncing all over the road like we are driving over some deep ruts, and the truck feels like it is at a vertical slant. We must be going down a very steep incline.

He has stopped the truck, and I can feel the cab door opening and shutting. He is unbolting the truck doors and pulling down the ramp. It is still dark outside, but as the lightning strikes, I can see the dark shadows of the tall trees and brush surrounding the truck. He is walking toward me. He has filled a syringe with his gloved hands and is jabbing the needle into my arm!

"There, Miss Shelby, I have given you a large amount of a great mind-altering drug. It has certainly paid for me to know all the right people on the streets. The drug should make the games that I am going to play with you much more exciting.

"You need to be catheterized again. When I am finished, I am going to take the straps off your ankles and wrists. I will help you get up on your feet so that I can walk you down the ramp.

"Alright, now that we are out of the truck, spread your feet apart and raise your arms above your head so that I can run my hands down your naked body and feel every part of you. Now turn your back to me and bend over a little so I can feel and look at your nice ass. Hold still so I can push my body against yours and thrust back and forth."

As he turns my body around so that I am facing him again, he squeezes me firmly by my shoulders and then grabs my hair.

"Undo the button on my pants and pull the zipper down. Now reach in and feel me so that you will know what you have to look forward to. Continue to stroke and play with me so I can get

27

primed for our little game, and tell me that you want this in you as badly as I do!"

He is yanking on my hair harder and screaming at me!

"Say it now!"

I am trying to get out the words that he so desperately wants to hear, but my voice is weak and trembling. As he pulls my hand away from his opened pants, he lets go of my hair.

"Now, Shelby, I am going to give you one chance to get away from me. Are you ready to run? I will count to thirty before I start hunting you down. One-two-three---"

I turn and begin to run as fast as I can through the dense timber. The branches and twigs are cutting into my bare feet, and the trees are starting to look as though they are intertwining. I can hear his wicked laugh as he shouts the numbers, "Thirteen - fourteen."

This is my one chance to stay alive. I feel like I am starting to run in slow motion. My arms and legs feel heavy, and I can hear his voice echoing in my head as he is counting. I can still envision his evil mask. The rain is trickling down my body, and I feel like I am gasping for every breath. There is nowhere to hide; all I can do is keep running. "Ouch!" I tripped and fell over a tree branch. "Oh, God, please, please." I have to get up and keep running or he will catch up with me. My leg and arm are bleeding, and now I am starting to see dark shadows of images appearing around and between the trees and weeds. The limbs on the trees are reaching toward me like long tentacles slicing at my bare skin.

As my eyes shift upwards and to the right I see flashing lights through the trees up ahead. The colors appear to be lights like those on a police car. I glance behind me as I run, and he is not there. "Oh, God, please let me get to that car for help." I am struggling to breathe, and my mouth is very dry. As I keep running, I finally reach a steep hill by a dirt road; I reach down to grab the weeds to help pull myself up the incline. "Oh, God, thank you! I see an unmarked police car!" I rush to open the door of the car. The man inside turns and looks at me, and I can see his satanic mask and hear his cruel, evil laugh.

I turn around quickly, lose my balance, and slide down the wet embankment. As I struggle to get back up on my feet, I hear his car door slam shut. I keep running straight ahead as fast as I can, knowing that he is just a short distance behind me.

Visions of many disembodied spirits of women have started to appear between the trees and all around me. The shadowy apparitions must be those of the women that he has murdered, or I am hallucinating from the drugs.

The sky is starting to get lighter, and I don't know how much longer I can keep running. Wait! I can see the outline of a large building up ahead. "Keep running, just keep running!" He is close behind me now. If I can just make it to that building, maybe there will be a place inside for me to hide.

With just a short distance to go, I see a large hole in the wall of this old, gray, abandoned building. As I reach the building I run through the opening and hear a loud bang. I turn around to see a steel-barred cell door slam shut behind me! He is standing on the other side of the door with his gloved fingers wrapped around the bars, staring at me.

"Oh, God, where can I hide from this beast?" I keep running as fast as I can down a long, dark hallway, and as the hall turns to the right, I round the corner. He is standing there waiting for me! As he reaches out and grabs me by my hair, he starts to laugh.

"We have reached our destination!"

Chapter Five - The Investigation Continues

There is someone knocking at the door. "Oh Peggy, come in and give me a hug. I am so glad you are here. Let me take your suitcase to my spare bedroom. Just go ahead and have a seat in the living room. I will be right there."

"Thanks, Ann. Have you heard anything from Shelby?"

"No, I'm afraid not. Can I get you a cup of coffee or something to drink?"

"No, I am so upset; I can't eat or drink anything. All I've done is cry. When Shelby didn't call me like she said she would, I knew in my heart that something was wrong."

"Hang on a minute Peggy; let me see who is at the door."

"Miss Parker? May I come in?"

"Yes, Deputy Taylor, please come in and have a seat in the living room. This is Shelby's mom, Peggy Grey. She just arrived a few minutes ago and will be staying with me for the next few days."

"Mrs. Grey, I'm Deputy Ron Taylor. I tried to call you on your home phone, but did not get an answer. Since you're both here, I would like you to follow me to the Sheriff's Department so I can ask you both a few questions. I know how upset you are Mrs. Grey, but I assure you that we will do everything we can to locate your daughter. Here is one of my cards so you will be able to reach me whenever you need to, day or night. I will see myself to the door, and we will talk more at the department."

As Ann closes the door behind him and turns around, we both begin to cry. "Ann, I can't believe this is all happening. I feel so lost and helpless. I was supposed to have lunch with Shelby today to celebrate her birthday. We need to grab my car keys and our purses; I'm sure the deputy is waiting in his car for us so that we can follow him."

As I drive, very few words are said. I can tell Peggy is in deep thought, and I just don't seem to know what to say to her.

The deputy has stopped in front of the building, and after getting out of his county car, he is standing there waiting for us to join him.

"Ladies, let's go inside, and you can follow me to a conference room. Please have a seat, and we will get started. This is a very difficult situation, Mrs. Grey. Your daughter has only been missing since last night, and at this time there is no proof of any foul play. We will be unable to file a missing person's report at this time. Her car has been impounded, and her car keys, purse and cell phone have been bagged and sealed and turned over to Detective Ryan Morse. Since you are both here, we would like to get you both fingerprinted."

"Miss Parker, I need to know approximately what time Shelby left the club, and was she alone at this time?"

"I believe, sir, that it was between 8:00 and 8:30 p.m., and yes, she left the club alone. We offered to walk her to her car, but she refused."

"Did she have any drinks containing alcohol?"

"Maybe one glass of wine; Shelby is not a drinker."

"Can you tell me what Shelby was wearing the night of the party?"

"Yes sir, she was wearing a pretty burgundy floral dress. It was sleeveless and was a little shorter than knee length. Her high heeled shoes were also the same burgundy color, and she had on a gold locket that she always wears around her neck."

"Mrs. Grey, do you have a recent picture of your daughter?"

"Yes sir, I have one here in my purse. Let me get it out of my wallet for you."

"Thank you. I will have to keep it in her file for awhile. Was your daughter dating anyone?"

"Not to my knowledge, but you know how young girls are; they don't tell their mothers everything."

"Ann, you're Shelby's best friend; do you know if she was dating anyone?"

"No sir, Shelby was very consumed with her work and didn't really date that much."

"Ann, would you be able to give me a list of the guests that attended her birthday party?"

"Yes, sir, that shouldn't be a problem."

There is a light tap on the door, and a tall, handsome, middle-aged man with gray hair enters the room. As Deputy Taylor stands up he says, "Detective Morse, this is Mrs. Grey, Shelby Grey's mother, and Shelby's best friend Ann Parker. I was just getting some information from them for my report."

"Mrs. Grey and Miss Parker, I apologize for the interruption, but I need to talk to Deputy Taylor out in the hall. We will be back in just a minute."

"Deputy Taylor, I checked Shelby's cell phone and found this disturbing picture of a naked girl strapped to a bed. I printed it out. I believe this is Shelby Grey in the picture, and we will have to confirm this with her mother. It is not going to be an easy thing to do, but we need to go back into the room and show her this picture."

As Detective Morse and Deputy Taylor enter the room, we both look up and can tell by the look on their faces that something is wrong.

"Mrs. Grey, I am going to have to show you a picture that I printed from your daughter's cell phone. I am sorry, but is this your daughter?"

"Oh God, it's her! It's Shelby! The locket that's around her neck was a gift from her dad. Since his death a year ago, she has worn it every day.

Who would do this to my daughter? Do you think she is still alive?"

"Mrs. Grey, I know that seeing this picture has to be very hard for you. Can we get you a glass of water? Detective Morse and I are going to step out of the room for awhile to give you and Ann some time alone. We will need to ask you both a few more questions when we return."

After they leave the room Peggy looks at me with tears rolling down her cheeks and says, "I feel like a piece of my heart has been torn out of my chest. I don't know what I would ever do without her. She is my whole life!"

After seeing that picture I can't imagine what Shelby went through, and I know that Peggy is devastated beyond words. I need to find a way to comfort her. Had I not had that party, this never would have happened!

"Peggy, we need to pray that they will find her and that she is still alive. We both need to cry our tears and just get it out of our system so that we can help Deputy Taylor and Detective Morse get the answers they need to start searching for her. Give me a hug, and remember that I will stay by your side and help you as much as I can. I love Shelby too; she is like a sister to me."

Deputy Taylor enters the room and places his hand on Peggy's shoulder before taking his seat at the table.

"Ladies, are you both able to answer a few more questions for me?"

"Yes, sir, we will do our best."

"Ann, did Shelby have any male friends that may have shown some interest in her?"

"No, sir, Shelby and I girl talked all the time. She would have told me."

"Did she say where she planned to go when she left the party?"

"Yes, she said she was going home to watch a movie or read a book. Shelby was not comfortable sitting in a bar."

"Was there anybody at that bar that may have said or done anything that you thought was out of the ordinary or that you might have felt was inappropriate?"

"No, we were all just a bunch of friends having fun together."

"Mrs. Grey, when was the last time you spoke to your daughter?"

"Shelby called me at about 6:45 last night while she was driving to the party. We were supposed to have lunch together today to celebrate her birthday. She didn't show up or call. I'm sorry sir; this is very difficult for me."

"I understand. I think you have both answered my questions for now. I will show you and Ann to the room where they can get your fingerprinting done. You both have my card; please call me if either of you thinks of anything else that you haven't already told me. We will keep you both informed on any updates that we get."

As we walk with the deputy to the other room, he says, "I'm sorry, Mrs. Grey, how long did you say that you would be staying in town?"

"I will probably go home in the next few days just to check my mail and pay a few bills that will be coming due."

As he opens the door to the room he says, "These gentlemen will be assisting you with your fingerprints. Thank you both for your time, ladies."

Chapter Six - His Playground

As he drags me by my hair down the long, dark hallway he laughs very loudly. "Did you enjoy our little game of chase?" I am so exhausted from the fear that he has put me through that my mind and body feel like they could shut down completely. I am terrified beyond words.

I can see small rooms with steel-barred cell doors enclosing each space on both sides of the hallway. The bluish gray paint on the cement floor is peeling, and the cement walls reek with a sickening smell of mold. I can hear faint crying and moaning sounds echoing throughout the hallways. This building embraces a powerful feeling of suffering and death. As we turn another corner, I see women on both sides of the hall who are confined in these rooms with torn and frayed padding on the walls. Some of these women are lying on cots, and some are pacing in their cells like caged wild animals. They are all staring at me as we pass by. This disgusting, demented man has created his own playground in an old abandoned mental hospital in the middle of nowhere.

"Dear God, how could he have committed this act of violence and abuse to this many women and never been caught? I know that he has buried a woman alive, but how many other women did he do this to? And where are they buried? Please God, I need your help!"

As we reach the end of the hall, he stops and releases my arm but still has a tight hold on my hair. He unlocks a padlock on a solid gray steel door and folds back the hinge. He pulls me into a large room with no windows. The walls look stained from the dampness, and it is dimly lit from an oil lamp hanging from a large rusty nail on the wall. In the middle of the room is a table with wheels that are locked into the floor, and there are leather belts and buckles bolted to each corner of the table. He tells me to get on the table and lie down, and he forces my arms up over my head and buckles my wrists into each belt. He then forces my legs apart and belts my ankles. He walks down to the end of the table and stands there looking at my body through that satanic mask.

"You will be cleansed, fed, and then given a drug-induced cocktail so that you will be able to better satisfy my needs. It has been a long wait!"

He turns and walks towards the door, then pauses and looks back at me before he shuts the door behind him. I can hear him latching and locking the door.

He has been waiting to sexually molest me this whole trip, and I am afraid the time has come for him to take his sickness out on me. I have to try to stay mentally strong so that I can fight him and find a way out of here. This can't really be happening! It has to be just a terrifying nightmare. "I am placing my life into your hands, God. Please help me!"

I have been lying here crying and shaking for at least two hours. I can see cameras attached to the wall on two corners of the room. I think this sick man is watching me on those cameras from another room, making me wait, knowing that the anticipation will make me more frightened than I already am.

I can hear him unlocking the padlock and pulling back the hinge on the door now. My heart is racing! The door is slowly opening, but it is not him! There is a woman walking toward me pushing a metal cart with one hand and carrying a basket over her other arm. As she pushes the cart up next to the table, I can see that the basket is full of dolls. They are propped up in the basket, partially covered with a dirty blanket. Some of them are missing hair, arms, or legs. They look like something out of a horror movie. The eyes on these dolls seem to be staring right at me.

The woman sets the basket of dolls on the floor next to the table and sorts through the items on her cart. She is wearing an old-fashioned black dress, and her pasty-white, badly scarred face is uncovered. She is breathing heavily with her mouth partially open, and the smell of her breath is sickening. Her long black hair is very thin, almost balding. As she uncovers the things on her cart, she is not making any eye contact with me at all.

Suddenly she turns toward me and places a clamp on my nose, forcing me to breathe through my mouth. After grabbing a catheter from the cart, she then reaches down and inserts it in me and holds a pan beneath me to catch the urine. She pours a pink liquid all over my body and dips a hard scrub brush into a pan of water. She begins to scrub my face and then moves the brush down over every part of my body. I can feel the hard bristles tearing at my skin causing it to feel like it's on fire. She reaches back to lift up the pan of cold water and dumps it all over my face and body. Grabbing a dirty rag, she starts blotting the water that runs off of me and then places the rag back on the metal cart.

Now she cups her hand to scoop something that looks like coarsely ground raw meat out of a bowl and forces the bloody stuff into my mouth. I cannot breathe with my mouth full, so I have to chew fast and swallow it so that I won't choke! She reaches over to lift a glass full of liquid to pour into my mouth. It runs down my throat and drips out of the corners of my mouth. When she bends over me, removing the clamp from my nose to place it back on her cart, I can smell her dress. It smells old – as though it had been in storage for many years.

She still has not spoken a word and has never looked into my eyes. After bending over to pick up her dolls, she pushes the cart back toward the door and walks out. I hear her closing and latching it.

"Dear God, where did this woman come from? Is she somebody that might have earned her freedom from a gated room? I feel so very sick! Please God, help me!"

I am becoming very light headed and can feel the muscles in my body starting to relax. Suddenly he appears out of nowhere, seeming to move from one side of me to the other and then above me as if he is floating like a large mass of vapor! The pain that I had been experiencing in my wrists and ankles no longer exists. I have a sense of euphoria; I feel like I don't give a damn about anything anymore.

Chapter Seven - New Evidence

"Hello."

"Hi, Ann. It's Peggy. I'm calling to let you to know that I just got home and wanted to thank you again for letting me stay at your place for the last several days."

"Peggy, I was glad you were here with me."

"I'm very tired, but I'm afraid I am not going to be able to sleep. The thought of my daughter being tied up to a bed naked and nobody knowing where she is or if she is still alive is more than any mother could stand. I just can't quit crying. I'm going to have to call my doctor in the morning to see if I can get something for my nerves, or I am not going to be able to get through all of this."

"I know, Peggy; I can't stop thinking about Shelby either. I had to go back to work this morning, and several people from work that attended her party said that they were called in to the Sheriff's Department for questioning. None of us are able to get any rest; we are all in such disbelief about the whole thing."

"Ann, if I can get in to see the doctor in the morning, sort through all of this mail, and get some bills paid, would you mind if I came back to stay with you for awhile? Being an only child myself and not having my parents and Shelby's dad here anymore I don't have anybody left to help me get through all of this, and I know that I can't do this by myself. I'm just not able to think straight nor do I feel strong enough."

"Peggy, I think it would be easier on you, me, and the Sheriff's Department if you did come back to stay with me. Why don't you call me in the morning before I leave for work? I usually leave here about 8:00 a.m. Try to get some rest, and I will talk to you in the morning."

"Thanks, Ann. I don't know what I would do without you. Maybe if I can eat something and lie down I will feel a little better. I will call you in the morning."

I need to take a shower and try to get some sleep myself. I can't even begin to imagine what Shelby is going through. Just thinking about the picture that Detective Morse showed us makes me physically sick. "Please God, protect my friend, and please let her still be alive."

The alarm just woke me, and I feel like I just went to sleep. I need to get up and make some strong coffee and wait for Peggy to call. When I turn on the TV, the local news station is broadcasting live from the Five Mile Roundup parking lot. The news reporter is saying that Shelby may possibly have been abducted from there and that if anyone has any information pertaining to the case, they should call the local Sheriff's Department. Seeing her picture posted on the television screen makes this horrible nightmare become a reality.

As I begin dressing for work, I can hear my cell phone ringing in the kitchen. That has to be Peggy.

"Hello."

"Hi, Ann. It's Peggy. I was awake half the night and can't stay focused on anything. I'm going to call the doctor at 9:00 a.m. to see if he can get me in, and when I get home from there I will pack my suitcases. If I throw all of my mail in a bag and bring it with me, would you have time to help me go through my bills? I am unable to concentrate on anything."

"I can help you with it, Peggy. I just decided while getting dressed that I'm going to take a personal day from work, so don't worry about it. When you get here we will go through your bills together. If the doctor gives you any medicine, be sure to ask him if it's safe for you to drive. I will see you when you get here. Drive safely!"

I feel so bad for Peggy; I can't even begin to imagine what she is going through right now. She didn't mention anything about seeing the news broadcast about Shelby on TV this morning. It's probably for the best. I'm going to call my boss and let him know that I'm using a personal day and then finish getting myself dressed. I probably should get a meal fixed for us to have for dinner tonight and then straighten up the house.

The day seems to have gone by very quickly; it is already 2:00 p.m. Peggy should be getting here soon. I am struggling with my emotions, and I just feel so helpless. Oh, there is somebody knocking on the door. It must be Peggy.

"Oh God, Peggy, come in. Are you going to be all right? Were you able to get in to see your doctor? Here, let me help you with your suitcases. Have a seat at the kitchen table, and I will get us a glass of tea or something to drink."

"Thanks, Ann. The doctor gave me a prescription for my anxiety, but he wants me to take it closer to evening. Have you heard anything from the Sheriff's Office?"

"No, but they did have the story on the news today, so I know they are working on things. Maybe someone at the club saw something that will help in their search for Shelby. Did you bring your mail so that we can go through it and get your bills figured out? I thought maybe we could just talk and relax for awhile and then sort through your mail so you're not worrying about it. I have dinner ready to put in the oven. We can eat a little later."

"Yes, it's all here in this bag. I can get my checkbook out when you are ready and write out checks as we go through the bills. There is also a padded envelope here that is postmarked from Kentucky that I haven't opened yet. I just threw everything in the bag. I constantly get junk mail. Do you have a pair of scissors that I can open it with?"

"Sure, let me grab them out of my desk drawer. Do you want me to open it for you?"

"Thanks, Ann. Go ahead while I am sorting through all these bills and junk mail."

"Peggy, there is a disc in here but no note or letter of advertisement with it. Companies send this kind of thing out all of the time to get people to sign up for stuff. I'm going to go into the living room and put it in my DVD player just to see if it is an advertisement. If it is, then we can just throw it away."

Oh my God! It's a recording of Shelby! I need to take it out before Peggy sees it and call Deputy Taylor. As I walk back into the kitchen crying and shaking, I know I have to tell her. "Peggy, when I put the disc into the DVD player, Shelby was on the recording. I don't think either of us should watch it. We need to call the Sheriff's Office right now." I grab the phone and punch in the number.

"County Sheriff's Office, Deputy Taylor speaking."

"Deputy Taylor, this is Ann Parker. Shelby's mom is back in town and is staying here with me again. She received a disc in the mail that had Shelby on it. I think you need to see this! Can you come over right away?"

"Yes, Ann, I will be right over. I will have Detective Morse come with me. Please put the disc and envelope down, and don't handle it again. We will be there right away!"

When I get off the phone with Deputy Taylor, Peggy asks what I had seen on the disc. After I cry and cry, I tell her that the disc did show that Shelby is still alive! Peggy then begins to weep, and I put my arm around her.

As Peggy calms down, there is a knock at the door. "Peggy, could you get the door for me? It is probably Deputy Taylor and Detective Morse. I need to use the bathroom."

When Peggy opens the door, Detective Morse is standing there. "Come in, sir."

"Thank you, Mrs. Grey. Deputy Taylor was called out to an accident on a county road. Can you show me where the disc and envelope are?"

"Ann set them on the table over there for you. She says she thinks Shelby is still alive."

"Mrs. Grey, I will have to bag and seal both of these items. After the disc is watched we will determine where to go from there. Did you receive these in the mail?"

"Yes, they were in with my mail when I returned home yesterday."

"What day did you receive them?"

"I was here with Ann for several days, so I'm not sure what day they were actually delivered."

"We have both sets of fingerprints from you and Ann, so these items will be brushed for any other prints. Thank you, Mrs. Grey. We will keep you informed."

"Peggy, was that Detective Morse?"

"Yes, he picked up the envelope and DVD."

"Good. Let's finish going through your mail so you can write out checks. We will get this all mailed off in the morning. When we are finished we can fix our plates and sit down to eat. I will clean up the kitchen after we are done eating, and you should try to get some rest. Don't forget to take your medicine before you lie down."

Chapter Eight - Fulfillment

She is unconscious from the drug that she was given. I can now begin to release all of the strong sexual needs that have been escalating inside of my mind and body for days. She is lying as still as a corpse, and that alone mentally and physically excites me.

I'm starting a video recorder; I want to be sure to capture everything that I do to her body on tape so that I can make a DVD to play back for her when she is conscious. Much of the enjoyment for me will follow later when I can watch her reaction and see the fear in her face when she sees what I have done to her body. Having released her wrists and ankles from the belts and buckles earlier will allow me to move her body freely into any position necessary to create a much better video and will definitely make it much more pleasurable for me while performing sex with her.

As I face the recorder, I am removing all of my clothes and running my hands down my body. I begin to feel and stroke myself and sense the excitement and anticipation of what is about to follow. I'm walking back toward her and

54

positioning myself so that when I begin to play with her body and place my penis inside of her vagina and then up her ass it will all be captured on tape. I will pace myself by using sexual toys on her in between to make this special time alone with her last as long as I possibly can.

After hours of gazing at every inch of her body and molesting her in every position possible, I have once again accomplished relieving myself from all of the sexual tensions I have been carrying inside of me. I am very anxious to watch what I have recorded over and over again. I am now ready to move her to a cell.

My eyelids feel heavy, and tears are rolling out of the corners of my eyes and running down my face and neck. I am lying on a small bed, and my wrists and ankles are no longer restrained to a table. My head is pounding, and I feel like I am going to throw up. I'm too dizzy and weak to even try to pull myself up into a sitting position. The private parts of my body are burning and throbbing from pain. My breasts ache, and my nipples are raw and bleeding. I can see deep purple bruised handprints on the tops of each of my thighs.

"Dear God, I am hurting so badly! How did I get from that large room to this cell, and what did he do to my body that would have caused this much pain? Please help me; I am so afraid!"

There is a dimly lit oil lamp hanging from a bracket on the wall in the hallway. I can see him roaming back and forth outside my cell door and looking at me. "Please God, I know he has been empowered by Satan, and I need you to protect me from him. He is trying to take possession of my soul by taking away my mental and physical strength."

I can feel myself drifting in and out of sleep. Flashbacks of me running away from him in the dark timber and terrifying thoughts of what he did to my body continue to flow in and out of my mind.

As I open my eyes again I can see the woman who scrubbed my body and forced food and liquid down my throat standing over me. She is placing her basket of dolls on the end of my bed and is removing a bottle of water from the pocket of her apron. She is reaching her hand underneath my neck and lifting up my head and pouring the water into my mouth. As she lowers my head back down she reaches with her other hand to touch my necklace. "Oh God, Daddy, help me please!"

She is picking up her basket of dolls and walking to the cell door. She has opened it and walked into the hall and is turning back around to lock it leaving me alone again.

"God, is this woman that freely roams the halls the way I can escape from here? Is she the answer to my prayers?"

She has turned the lamp off in the hallway. As I lie here in the dark in pain and fear, I can hear other women screaming and crying as if they are being tortured.

I must have fallen into a deep sleep again for many hours; it is much lighter in here now. I know that he has managed to fill me full of drugs and has brutally exploited every inch of my body.

As I look up, I can see a large black spider on the ceiling in the corner above my bed. It is busy weaving a large web. The insects that it will trap will be like me - completely unable to fight off what is trying to take away our existence.

"Daddy, I have been praying. I know you can see me, and you know what he has done to me. Please watch over me and protect me from this disgusting animal."

Chapter Nine - Unearthing a Nightmare

"911, what is your emergency?"

"Oh God, please, I need help right away!"

"Miss, please try to calm down. Can I have your name and the reason for this emergency call?"

"My name is Donna Pratt. I am in the Country Church Cemetery on Radcliff Road. I'm standing by my husband's grave, and something is horribly wrong!"

"Mrs. Pratt, are you experiencing physical difficulty? Do you need an ambulance dispatched?"

"No, please, I need you to get somebody to help me! My husband was buried here four days ago, and there are hundreds of flies everywhere, flying in the air and crawling on the ground. There are small worms slithering all over his grave. The smell is unbearable, and animals, or something, have been digging holes in the ground. It looks like there is a piece of human flesh sticking out of the dirt that is covering his grave!"

"Mrs. Pratt, please stay on the phone with me while I radio the Clark County Sheriff's Department. I have dispatched them to assist you. Are you still on the line?"

"Yes, I'm still here, but I am feeling nauseous and shaky, and I am scared, very scared!"

"Mrs. Pratt, please try to calm down so I can clearly understand what you are saying. Are you sure you don't need an ambulance dispatched?"

"No, I just need somebody to please come and help me!"

"Mrs. Pratt, someone should be arriving there soon. Are you still standing at your husband's graveside?"

"No, I just walked away, and I am sitting in my car. I am shaking all over. Oh, please, will help be coming soon? My husband was just laid to rest; I can't believe this! Wait, I can see the lights on the county cars turning into the cemetery now. I need to get off the phone!"

Three county cars have pulled into the narrow, graveled road inside the cemetery and are pulling in behind my car to park. The officers are getting out of their cars and walking toward me. As I'm trying to stand up to get out of the car, I start to feel light headed, and as I stagger a little, one of the deputies catches me by my arm.

"Miss, why don't you sit back down in your car? Could you please give us your name and identification?"

"My name is Mrs. Donna Pratt, and I will get my license out of my purse for you. Here it is; please help me! My husband's grave is right over there, and something is very wrong! You need to do something!"

"Mrs. Pratt, I will stay here with you while the detective and the sheriff walk over to your husband's grave."

As they return to the car, the sheriff asks me if there is anyone I can call to give me a ride home. He can see the emotional state that I am in and that I should not be driving my car.

"Mrs. Pratt, we will need to close off this area, so if you don't have anybody that you can call, I will have Deputy Patterson give you a ride home. I am Sheriff John Wright, and here is one of my cards. We will need you to pull your car off to the side a little more. We will then need to get some questions answered so that we can start a report.

"Sheriff Wright, I would feel better if your deputy would take me home. I am terrified from seeing my husband's grave in this condition, and I'm not feeling well at all."

"Deputy Patterson, can you please help Mrs. Pratt to your county car and take her home? You can begin questioning her and get the report started. Just check back in to the department when you are finished."

As we drive out of the cemetery, all I can do is cry. It was painful enough to lose my husband of twenty- two years, but then to come to the cemetery with intentions of watering the flowers on his grave and saying some prayers, and to find this horrible sight! God, this is terrible!

"Detective Weiser, we need to block off the entrances and exits to the cemetery right away and tape off this entire area. I am going to radio for assistance from the State Police; this definitely is going to be more than we can handle. I will make sure that they are aware that we will need crime scene investigators as well as notifying the Jeffersonville Coroner. I'm afraid we have a real mess on our hands! Being such a small community, who would have ever guessed we would be facing such a nightmare? I will grab the tape so we can start securing the area. The State Police and the investigators should be arriving soon. Detective, in all my years of being the Sheriff, I have never seen anything quite this bad. Well, Detective, it looks like the state troopers and the CSI team are arriving now. We will need to assist them in any way we can."

"Sheriff Wright? I am Agent Nathan Miller from Crime Scene Investigation; I will be overseeing my team."

"Thank you for your quick response. This is Detective Weiser from the Clark County Sheriff's Department who will be working with you. What do you need us to do?"

"We will need to set up a couple of tents and tables. After the team suits up we will have to secure any dirt that we remove from the grave in these barrels and filter through each scoop of dirt, one at a time, for any evidence. Other team members will be using digital and film cameras with various lenses, flashes, and filters. They will also be doing sketches and recording measurements. After the corpse has been carefully uncovered we will be gathering blood samples, lifting hair samples, and collecting any physical evidence before wrapping the body. We will also need your help making sure that no one gets into this area. Although it is a small country cemetery, news travels fast, and we don't want any reporters or other news people near here! If you will excuse me, we need to get to work."

"Detective Weiser, let's help them get these tents and tables set up. It looks like the State Police officers have the cemetery entrances and exits well covered and secured. I think it's going to be a long, gruesome afternoon!"

"Sheriff Wright and Detective Weiser, we will need you to put on these gloves before handling the tables."

I see that the teams taking photos and precise measurements and the rest of the team have already put on their suits, gloves, and helmet- type masks. This group of crime scene investigators works very quickly and really knows what they are doing. I have been a sheriff for many years but have never had to exhume a body from a grave. Oh, here comes a State Trooper walking toward Detective Weiser and me now.

"Sheriff, there are so many ways for the public to access this area besides the entrances and exits, that we will need you and your detective to help us watch for anyone trying to enter the cemetery. Until this situation is fully under control and the job is completed, we know we will need you to assist us."

"Not a problem; we just finished setting up the tables for the CSI team. I am Sheriff Wright, and this is Detective Weiser from the Clark County Sheriff's Department."

"I am Sergeant Durick. Sheriff Wright, I think maybe we should line all of the county cars and patrol cars up on the other side of the cemetery to help keep everyone out. This side is all fenced with a field of hay beyond it."

"Sounds good. We will get our county cars moved over to that area now."

After many grueling hours of bagging and sealing evidence, Agent Miller and his team are placing bags over the feet and hands of a woman who was in the very shallow grave and wrapping the body in a white cloth. She is now being placed into a body bag and will be moved to the county morgue where the medical examiner and coroner will complete the autopsy to determine the cause of death.

After taking her body to their vehicle, Agent Miller approaches all of us. He states that their work here is complete and that they will be present at the morgue for the autopsy in order to take additional pictures or video footage as well as collecting tissue samples from the major organs of her body for analysis at the crime lab. He asks that we notify the cemetery groundskeeper right away to have him bring in more dirt for the grave to replace what they had to keep in the barrels to be analyzed. He also asks Detective Weiser and me if we could remain here until the job is finished.

As the troopers leave the cemetery, the crime scene investigators follow behind them with her body. I just placed the call to the groundskeeper, and we will wait here until the job is completed. It has been a very long, nerve-racking day. I am still struggling with the fact that this happened in our small community.

Chapter Ten - Showtime

While lying in bed, I can feel the pain pulsating through my body and my mind continuing to drift from one thought to another. I silently talk to God and my dad through my prayers and think about how good my life was before being abducted by this very sick man. I find myself trying to block out the fear that lies deep within my mind by replacing it with pleasant thoughts of my childhood.

I can picture my mom standing at the stove cooking for Dad and me as we patiently waited at the table for our food to be served. We could smell all of the wonderful aromas throughout the kitchen as she was preparing our meal. After she placed the food on the table and sat down, we would all join hands as a family and thank God for our blessings.

As I wipe the tears that are streaming down my face, I can hear the faint thumping of wheels on the cement floor. As the sound increasingly becomes louder, I know that whatever is making this noise is getting closer and closer to me. I look over, and she is standing outside of my cell with her metal cart in front of her and her basket of dolls hanging over her arm.

"Please dear God, don't let this be a repeat of her preparing my body for that sick demon to once again molest me. My body is too weak to have any more pain inflicted upon it. God, who is this woman, and how did she manage to survive?"

She is unlocking the cell door and entering the room. She pushes her cart toward me. After placing her basket of dolls at the end of my bed, she reaches into a pan of soapy water on her cart and rings out a dripping wet rag with her hands. Unlike before, she is gently wiping off the blood from all of my cuts and scratches and is thoroughly washing every inch of my body.

I'm watching her as she is cleansing me. "Please, why won't you look at me or talk to me?" She has her head hanging down as though she is ashamed. Her eyes and facial expressions give me a sense that she is very sad, scared, and lonely. She turns and looks toward my face and begins to open her mouth very wide, almost as if she is going to scream. Oh my God! She is showing me that the front half of her tongue is missing! What has this demon put her through, and why did he spare her from death to roam the hallways?

As she is reaching down to touch my necklace again, I slowly lift my hand up and gently place it on top of hers. She abruptly jerks her hand away and reaches towards the end of my bed to grab her basket of dolls. She quickly turns back around and places her hands on the cart, starting to push it toward the cell door. She stands in the hallway looking from side to side as if she is afraid of being seen or caught by somebody. Leaving her cart sit, she walks back toward me again and reaches into her apron pocket after glancing back over her shoulder. She quickly pulls out a slice of bread and a piece of rotten apple and hands them to me. Now she is turning hastily and walking through the doorway locking the door behind her.

"Please help me!" She continues to walk away and is no longer in sight.

I am devouring the bread and piece of brown apple like an animal. I am so hungry and sick to my stomach from not having anything to eat that I'm barely chewing the food before swallowing it.

"God, I just know that she has to be the answer to my prayers and that she could help me to escape from here. What other reason would she have for giving me some fruit and bread and washing my body gently like a mother would wash her child? Why does she carry those damaged dolls? Was she abducted by him as a child and out of some strange sort of remorse he allowed her to keep them?"

As I close my eyes to rest, I can hear his wicked voice loudly calling, "Shelby, oh Shelby, I have a movie for you to watch!"

I open my eyes and hear his footsteps coming down the hallway toward my cell and hear his horrifying laugh. "Please God, help me!" He is unlocking my cell door and walking toward me. After reaching my bed, he stands above me looking at my naked body and reaches down and places his hand tightly around the top of my arm, forcing me up on my feet.

"Get up, Shelby; I am taking you to watch a movie. I have watched it several times and am anxious for you to see it.

I must say I am quite the producer and have captured the sexual moments in the movie very well! I am going to be leaving the building for three or four days, and I want you to have plenty to think about while I am gone."

"Mister, please stop pinching my arm. You're hurting me, and my body is in too much pain to walk."

"Come on, quit whining and keep walking!"

As we turn down another hallway, he stops to unlock a solid door and shoves me inside a dark room. There is a chair sitting in the middle of the room, and he forces me to sit down on it. He is now restraining my ankles and wrists to the chair with pieces of rope. There is a large white cloth hanging on the wall ahead of us, and to the right of my chair is an old cart with a projector and laptop computer sitting on top of it. Another chair sits next to the cart. After turning on the computer and inserting a DVD, he is taking a seat.

"Miss Shelby, it's showtime!"

As I look up at the images projected on the wall, I see him staring through his mask and removing his clothes. I see my naked body lying on a table behind him, unconscious. "Oh God, what is he doing to me? I can't watch this!"

"Open your eyes now, Shelby, and continue to watch this, or I will sew your eyelids open with a needle and thread. I worked very hard on this DVD, and you will watch it!"

As he begins to sprawl out in his chair with his arms lying over his stomach, he throws his head back and laughs hysterically.

"As I look at the fear in your eyes and the expressions on your face, I know I have succeeded. This gives me so much pleasure!"

The anger is building up in me like a volcano ready to erupt. I am being forced to watch what this satanic, insane man has done to my body. I want to lash out and hurt him as badly as he is hurting me. I'm feeling true hatred for the first time in my life, and it is causing my stomach to feel like it is knotting up. I am feeling very sick! I hate this gutless man that is hiding behind a mask!

After what seems to be several hours or more, the DVD has finally stopped playing. He reaches over to remove it from the laptop and is now holding up another DVD in his gloved hand. He laughs unmercifully.

"Surprise! I have a preview of coming attractions!"

Chapter Eleven - Inside the Morgue

My partner and I are on our way to the morgue with the remains of Jane Doe. I requested that the coroner's office contact a medical examiner to perform the autopsy. This job is going to require an expert in this field because it is definitely a homicide. Hopefully he will be there by the time we arrive at the morgue.

As we turn into the driveway and park the vehicle, a short, stout gentleman comes out of the building pushing a morgue gurney. I step out of the vehicle. "Coroner Gustafson?"

"Yes, you must be Agent Miller from CSI."

"Yes, sir, I am, and this is my partner Agent Greene. Has the medical examiner arrived yet?"

"Yes, he has; he is ready and waiting for us. Let's get her on the gurney and go inside so we can get her body prepared for the autopsy."

As we are taking her body down a long hallway, I think about this job. I can honestly say that it never becomes routine. I constantly find myself mentally justifying why I do this for a living. I know that what I do helps to bring closure for the loved ones of the deceased as well as uncovering critical evidence to bring justice to the victim, but it definitely is not your run-of-the-mill job.

When we reach the autopsy room, the medical examiner is standing by the table dressed in his scrubs with his facial mask tipped up. As he extends his arm out in front of him to shake my hand he says, "I presume you are Agent Miller? Just refer to me as Dr. Dan."

"Dr. Dan, this is my partner Agent Greene. We will put on our scrubs, plastic aprons, gloves, and facial shields and help you get Jane Doe out of the body bag and onto the table. Our other team members are transporting the evidence that we collected from the crime scene to the crime lab as we speak."

After carefully removing her from the body bag and slipping off the bags that cover her feet and hands, we fold back the white cloth that is draped over her naked body and use a board to slide her over to the table.

Dr. Dan has asked Agent Greene to take some photographs of the scars on numerous parts of her body: a birthmark on her upper left thigh, many areas that have been badly bruised, and her left hand where all of her fingertips are missing. After taking fingerprints of her right hand, he says, "Agent Greene, when you are finished, if you wouldn't mind, I will have you start logging and charting for us while we do this autopsy to make things go a little smoother and faster."

"I don't mind at all. I will take the photos you need now so you can get started."

"The body is that of a white female approximately thirty-two years of age. She measures five foot four and a half inches; her weight is one hundred ten pounds and four ounces. There is maggot activity, and her body is swollen from gasses. I would say she has been dead for about four days. I will take another blood sample to check her DNA, another hair sample to see if there are drugs in her system, and tissue samples from under her fingernails. Her eyes are badly hemorrhaged indicating suffocation, and there are no signs of trauma to the skull area. We now need to get x-rays to see if she has any broken or fractured bones.

"Agent Miller, take a look at these x-rays. It appears that she has some broken ribs and an older fracture to the bone in her right lower leg. It also appears that she has four spots on her large intestine.

"Agent Greene, please note that some of her teeth have been recently extracted, and there is bruising and swelling in the gum area. Her breasts have open cuts on them, and she has vaginal tissue scarring and tearing. We will have to swab her vaginal area for evidence.

"Well, gentlemen, it is time to make our Y incision and check out her internal organs. Agent Greene, could you get a picture of her rib cage to show the broken ribs prior to us splitting the ribs?"

"Yes, sir; I will get several pictures."

"We now need to examine her lungs and heart for any abnormalities. Then we can extract tissue and blood samples from these organs prior to measuring and weighing them. I will also remove a urine sample from her bladder. Agent Miller, it appears on the x-rays that her stomach is empty but is clouded from gas. I am, though, going to make an incision in the large intestine to see what those black marks are that show up on the x-ray.

"Gentlemen, it appears that there are four fingertips, with the nails attached, along with a piece of bone in each, lodged in her intestine. We will need to get DNA on each fingertip that we remove. Now we can measure and weigh the rest of her lower organs.

"I am ready to replace her organs and stitch her up. We will need to get her to the cooler as soon as possible. I will note that she has been badly sexually and physically abused over a long period of time. She is also malnourished, and the cause of death – suffocation.

"Excuse me while I take this call

"The report from the National Missing Persons System confirms that the fingerprints from our Jane Doe identify her as Margaret Lewis from Chicago, IL. Her family will have to be notified, and they will need to identify her from a picture and make arrangements to have her body moved to a funeral home.

"Agent Miller, the fingertips we removed from her intestine will be kept in an iced transporting container and taken to the crime scene lab for DNA testing."

Chapter Twelve - Coming Attractions

As I sit here feeling totally helpless, tied to a chair in this dark room, I can't even begin to comprehend the fact that he just forced me to watch what he did to my body while I was unconscious. He is now going to continue to mentally torture me by making me watch his sick version of coming attractions.

The power in this room embraces the presence of God and Satan at the same time. God is very much alive in my heart and mind, but Satan is once again unveiling more of his demonic acts through this hateful and sick man. The battle between God and Satan is being fought in this very room right here and now.

He is inserting the DVD into the computer and is sitting back in his chair looking as though he can't wait to watch his great filming abilities.

"Miss Shelby, it is time for coming attractions. I hope you get as much pleasure from watching this as I did from taping it."

As I look up at the sheet hanging on the wall, it is hard to describe the hatred that I am feeling. I can see him recording what is in front of him as he walks down a hallway and opens up a steel door.

He enters a room and walks toward what appears to be a thick, clear, plastic-enclosed box the size of a coffin that is held up off the floor by three old wooden saw horses. As he walks closer to it and zooms in with his recorder, I can see a tube running into the end of the box. He slowly moves the camera to the left, clearly capturing a view of a naked woman completely encased in this tightly enclosed space. The poor woman is covered with spiders the size of a quarter crawling all over her face and body. He is feeding just enough oxygen into the box to keep her and these horrifying insects alive. I can see one of his hands reaching out and tapping on the plastic case to stir up the spiders. He now appears to be above her filming down, and I see the fear in her face and the tears that are running out of the corners of her eyes and down her cheeks. Her body is completely covered with large, red welts from their bites.

"God, I know you can hear me. What possible reason does this man have that would cause him to inflict this much mental and physical pain on women? Is he hurting that badly inside that he has to hurt other people? Please help me to be prepared for the road that I have to travel yet, and protect these women who still have a path ahead of them to walk. I need some answers to be able to cope! That poor woman who was in that plastic-like coffin was thin; she had auburn colored hair and was so young! She could not have been over twenty years old. Why, God, is this all happening?"

He must have been dangling the camera down as he was walking because I can see the cement floor and occasionally the bottom of his pant leg and his shoe. He lifts the camera up as he enters another room. He is filming an extremely thin girl with curly brown hair who is naked and completely covered with blood. Her hands are strapped to metal bars that are cemented into the wall. Her arms are holding the weight of her body because she is so limp and barely able to stand up on her feet.

He has shifted the camera, and I can see, dangling in front of the woman, a large steel hook with a piece of meat on it hanging from a thick rope attached to the ceiling. As he moves the camera in closer, I can see razor blades sticking out all over this piece of meat.

He shifts the camera back to her face and moves closer to her. Oh my God, there are deep cuts all over her face and tongue with blood streaming out of them and down her body! Is this what he did to the woman who roams the halls? I can hear him laughing again, and he is saying to her, "Food for thought, no pun intended, but wouldn't it be less painful for you to starve than to bleed to death?"

I am feeling very faint and tears are streaming down my face. As I look over at him, I can see his eyes staring at me through his mask.

"What, Miss Shelby? Are you impressed with my creative filming talents? You're only seeing a small portion of the hell I have created for all of you! I have eighteen girls in captivity now, you included, and that does not take into consideration the women who weakened and are now buried!"

"Mister, you are going to burn in hell and forever be tormented by demons! You are the weak one, hiding behind your mask! You may be able to control my body while you have me strapped down or shock my mind into a constant state of fear by showing me how truly mentally unstable you are through your actions and sick DVD's, but you will never have control of my soul. God created my soul and protects and cradles me in his arms. You are possessed by Satan!"

He is jumping up from his chair and quickly walking toward me. He places his hands tightly around my throat and stares into my eyes as he is choking me! Now he suddenly releases his hands from my neck and steps away from me shouting, "I won't kill you because that is exactly what you want so that you won't have to be tortured or in pain!"

He walks back to the computer and reaches down to remove the DVD. He is now stepping back toward me and squatting down to release my ankles from the chair and to cut the rope from my wrists.

"Get up on your feet you little bitch!"

He is squeezing the top of my arm tightly and forcing me back through the door and down the hallway. As we reach my cell, he unlocks the door, shoves me in, and forcefully pushes me down onto the bed. He is standing above me pointing his finger at my face. "I am leaving the building now to abduct my next victim to once again satisfy my sexual needs. There aren't any to bury this trip, so I will be back within four or five days."

Out of nervousness and desperation, I am laughing out loud at him as he is walking toward the cell door. As he is in the hall locking the door, he says to me, "You better do a lot of praying to your God because I am going to soon own your soul!" He is walking away and is soon out of site.

"Dear God, I am trembling all over, and I am so afraid. He is in search of another victim, and I need you to stop him. Please help to ease the pain that he has inflicted upon on all of us that are held in captivity, and give us the strength we will need to fight him."

Chapter Thirteen - Findings from the Lab

There is a tap on the door and as I look up, the door is opening.

"Sergeant Durick, I have all the test results from the crime scene lab and a copy of the autopsy report on Margaret Lewis. May I come in?"

"Yes, Agent Miller. Let's take a seat at the table."

"Well, Sergeant Durick, Margaret Lewis was from Chicago, Illinois, and has been missing for a little over two months. The reports show that there were several types of street drugs in Margaret's body. There was no DNA sample found underneath her fingernails, but there were, however, small fiber samples found on different parts of her body, from her feet to the top of her head, during the examination at the crime scene. It appears that she was wrapped in some type of material before she was placed into that shallow grave. If you look at these three pictures, you can see the bruising on the tops of her thighs, and during the examination we found vaginal tears and scars, but there was no DNA found from the swab that was taken.

"Sir, we were able to lift a set of fingerprints from her body, and after processing them through the system, we found them to be that of Shelby Grey from Nashville, Tennessee, who has also been listed on the Missing Persons Database for about one week. This is a recent picture of her.

"All of the scars and open cuts that appear in these pictures were examined and checked for any particles that may have been imbedded into them, but there were no findings other than dirt from the grave. On the x-rays we found broken ribs and an old fracture to her right lower leg. We also found four dark spots on her large intestine.

"Please look very closely at this photo. It shows the remains of four fingertips that we removed from her large intestine. From testing the samples of bone fragments and tissue that were inside the fingers, it was determined through DNA that they are from four different women, all of whom are also listed on the National Missing Persons database. These are the photos of those women. This one is Mary Gibbs from Cedar Falls, Iowa; this one is Jody Taylor from Hazel Green, Wisconsin; the following picture is Patsy Harkness from Davenport, Iowa; and this picture is Carolyn

Nickerson from Portage, Indiana. These four women all range from eighteen years of age to twenty-six years of age. Some of them have been missing for over two years.

"This close-up photo of our victim shows the severe hemorrhaging in her eyes, which tells us that she was more than likely buried alive and suffocated from the dirt that she was covered with at the gravesite.

"Sergeant Durick, we are looking at five women from four different states that are still missing. All five women in some way are linked to this one homicide. I believe, sir, that at this point in time we need to call in the Federal Bureau of Investigation."

"Agent Miller, I appreciate all of the work you and your team have put into this case. I know you have all worked around the clock to compile this information as quickly as you did, and I appreciate it."

"I will leave all these copies with you, sir, so that you can read and study all of this information. I have also included a copy of the medical examiner's report. All of the evidence from the crime scene, photographs, and the footage that was filmed during the autopsy is being held at the crime scene lab. Please advise me if there is anything else you need from me and my team, and let me know how we can be of further assistance to you."

"Agent Miller, I will be going over all of this information, and I will keep you informed and call you when I have made a decision. Once again thank you and your team."

Well, it looks like I have a lot of paperwork to go through with a fine- toothed comb. I guess I will be here late into the night. It is obvious to me that we have a killer who is abducting women while traveling from state to state that needs to be taken off the streets.

As I lean back in my chair reading the reports that Agent Miller left with me, the phone rings and startles me. I pick up the phone, "Sergeant Durick speaking."

"Sergeant Durick, there are crew members from a local news station in the lobby. Could you please come out and talk to them?"

"Yes, I will be there right away."

As I am walking to the lobby I can see that they have their cameras and are filming live. The news broadcaster is saying, "Good evening folks, we are broadcasting live from the Clark

County State Police Department. Sergeant Durick, what do you have to say about the body that was removed from a shallow grave at the Country Church Cemetery located just off Radcliff Road?"

"Sir, we are unable to report anything at this time. The family members of the deceased have not all been notified yet."

"Sergeant Durick, we have been to the cemetery and have seen the grave. Obviously this was a homicide because the groundskeeper said that a local gentleman had been buried in that spot six days ago."

"No comment. I have nothing to report at this time. We will notify you about holding a news conference when we are ready to do so. Please leave the premises."

As I am walking back to my office, I can hear the news broadcaster say, "Folks, tune in to WIBA Channel 23 morning news for a follow-up on this story."

From my office door I can see that the reporters are leaving the building. It sure doesn't take long for news reporters to jump on a chance at a story. I think I am going to call it a night and continue reading the reports in the morning so that I can get back with Agent Miller on this case. On my way out I will ask the dispatcher to have one of our state patrol officers take a ride past Mrs. Pratt's house to make sure the news people are not harassing her.

Chapter Fourteen - Sorting Out My Thoughts

At least an hour or so has passed by, and I can only hope he has left the building. I do pray that he does not find another innocent woman to abduct.

I can sense that someone is staring at me. As I turn my head and look over to my left, she is standing at my cell door looking in at me. She does not have the cart she usually pushes in front of her, but she does have her basket of dolls hanging from one arm. She is holding out her apron as though she is carrying something in it. She shifts one corner of the apron over to the other hand to form a pouch as she unlocks the door and enters my room.

She is now walking toward me and bends forward to place her basket of dolls on the end of my bed. As she unfolds the pouch that she has formed with her apron, she shows me that she has an apple, a piece of bread, and a few berries. As I empty her apron and take the food, she takes a seat next to me on my bed. While I eat the apple, she strokes my hair with her hands.

"He told me he was leaving the building for three or four days. Could you please let me go for a walk in the hall with you?"

She pushes herself up from my bed onto to her feet and leans back over to pick up her dolls. She has made her way to the door and is standing in the hallway. She turns the key to lock the door behind her. Tears are running down my cheeks. "Thank you for the food. Please can't you help me get out of here?"

I do not understand what is happening. If he is away from the building, she should be helping all of us. Is she so afraid and in fear for her own life that she does not try to escape herself? I don't remember how I entered this building, but I do remember being drugged and chased through the timber. Maybe she tried to escape, and he tortured her by cutting off her tongue! "Please God, give me the strength I need to try to figure things out, and please help all of these other women who are being held against their will. Thank you for blessing me with something to eat."

I must have drifted off to sleep while I was praying but was just awakened by the distant sounds of frightful screams coming from inside this building. After watching a small portion of his sick coming attractions, I can't imagine what these women are going through physically and emotionally. I must find a way out of here!

"Please, God, help me to clear my mind so that I can think things through. I can't stand to hear these women scream in pain anymore. Why haven't the police apprehended him yet? I feel so helpless!"

I can hear the sound of the wheels on her cart thumping on the cement floor, getting closer and closer to my room. As I look up, she is standing outside my cell again. She unlocks the door and pushes her cart toward me. Turning around, she relocks the door.

Should I try to fight her to get the key away from her? As she stands in front of me while I sit up on the bed, she reaches down to pick up a pair of scissors from the cart. Oh God, is she going to stab me with them? She holds the scissors in one hand and reaches over with her other hand to clench chunks of my hair, cutting them off and placing them on the cart. Why is she cutting off all of my hair?

I look up at her with tears in my eyes. "Please help me to escape from here, and I promise I will get help for you and all these other poor women!"

She turns and walks away, pushing the cart full of hair. She has once again entered the hallway and is turning around to lock the door. I think she has been through so much pain and suffering that her mind is just gone. She is not going to be able to help me.

As I lie back down on the bed, I begin to sob. I know he will be returning to the building in a few days, and it will then be impossible for me to get out of this living hell.

Chapter Fifteen - Calling in the FBI

"Good morning, Sergeant Durick. You're here bright and early this morning. I just made a pot of strong coffee if you would like a cup."

"Thanks, Nancy. I may need more than just one cup to get me through the day. Could you hold all of my calls for me this morning? I know that I will be busy for the next several hours reading through the files that CSI Agent Miller dropped off to me last night."

"Not a problem, sir."

"Oh, and Nancy, could you send an officer out to check on Mrs. Pratt for me? Please stress to him that he needs to assure her that her husband's grave has been properly taken care of. Just buzz me if you need me."

"Yes, sir, I will do this right away."

As I am walking down the hall to my office, I can't help but think that this horrific crime could have happened to my wife or daughter. When an incident like this one hits this close to home, it does makes you stop and think.

Well, after a sip of hot coffee, I guess I will start by reading the autopsy report. According to the medical examiner's report, Margaret Lewis was raped and tortured over a several month span and then buried alive. These pictures clearly show she was brutally beaten and cut.

The missing persons report states that she was abducted from a parking lot at a department store in the outskirts of Chicago, IL. I remember seeing this picture cross my desk and seeing it on the news, but I would never have guessed that I would be involved in this investigation.

Going through any more of these reports would be a waste of precious time. Five of these woman could still be alive somewhere. I need to call the FBI headquarters in Washington, DC, immediately. I also need to call Agent Miller to let him know that I have made the decision to call in help on this case.

"CSI, Agent Nathan Miller speaking."

"Agent Miller, this is Sergeant Durick. I have placed a call to the FBI. They have agreed to fly a behavioral analysis unit here today. They have been assigned the task of this case and are fully aware that it involves a homicide that includes six different women from five different states. They will call me with an arrival time, and I will keep you informed."

"Thank you, Sergeant Durick. I will have individual copies of each report printed and ready for them by the time they arrive. I will be waiting for further instructions."

Noticing my blinking intercom button, I reach out and push it. "Yes, Nancy, how can I help you?"

"Sorry to bother you, sir, but I just received a call from Mrs. Pratt. She is very upset. She can't even step out of her house because of all the news reporters and their camera crews. They have set up equipment all over her yard."

"Nancy, please dispatch several officers to her location, and tell them to remove the reporters from her property. Have the officers tell the reporters that they will be notified where and when a news conference will be held."

"Yes, sir, consider it done."

As I sit here going through the autopsy pictures of Margaret Lewis, it makes me wonder how anyone could be this cruel to another human being. Her body is so horribly bruised and cut up.

The buzzer just startled me. "Yes, Nancy?"

"Sorry, sir. I know you are going to want to take this call on line one; it is the FBI headquarters."

I push the button and pick up the phone. "Sergeant Durick speaking. Yes, sir. OK, sir, I will notify Agent Miller of their arrival time. Thank you for your assistance."

"CSI, Agent Miller speaking."

"Agent Miller, this is Sergeant Durick. I have just been notified that the BAU unit will be arriving at your location at six o'clock central standard time. I will be present for the meeting and hope to be there prior to their arrival."

"Thanks for the update, sir. I will have everything ready by then."

I need to get all of the paperwork together from my office for tonight's meeting, and then I think I will swing by our house and spend some quality time with my wife and daughter. I look for it to be a late night. First I need to buzz Nancy.

"Yes sir?"

"Nancy, do I have any messages that need to be followed up right away?"

"No, sir."

"I'll be leaving the office soon. Did the officers take care of the problem at Mrs. Pratt's house?"

"Yes, sir, they did."

"Thanks Nancy. You know how to reach me if I'm needed."

"Have a good afternoon and evening, sir."

After spending time with my wife and daughter, I give each of them a hug and kiss goodbye. As I'm walking out the door, I remind my wife to lock the door behind me.

While driving to the CSI building, I think to myself what a lucky man I am to have such a nice family. I love them both, and I am very thankful!

The drive to the CSI building is a slow one because of all the after- work traffic, but I have allowed ample time to get there. I can't help but wonder if the person who committed this homicide is traveling on the same road that I'm on or if this person is possibly hiding out within our city.

As I am pulling into the parking lot, I glance down at my watch. It looks like the unit should be arriving here in about forty-five minutes. This will allow time to go over our reports and notes.

I can see Agent Miller walking toward me in the hallway as I enter the front door.

"Sergeant Durick, I see you found the building without a problem."

"Yes, Agent Miller. Traffic was heavy, but I allowed myself plenty of time to get here."

"We will need to stop here, and Elizabeth will get you signed in and issue you a visitor's badge. We will be holding the meeting in the large conference room at the end of the hall. If you would, just follow me."

As we enter the room, several men and women stand up, and then we all take a seat at the large table. Agent Miller begins the meeting. "We will begin going over our reports and notes to prepare for the arrival of the BAU. Sergeant, you are welcome to help yourself to some coffee. This meeting could be a lengthy one."

Time has quickly passed by when there is a knock on the conference room door. A young lady opens the door. "Agent Miller, the unit has arrived."

We all rise from our seats as the unit enters the room.

"Welcome to Indiana. We all appreciate your presence and are looking forward to assisting you with this case. I am CSI Agent Miller, and this is Sergeant Durick. The other men and women here are part of my team, and I am sure you will all become familiar with each other over the next few days."

"Nice to meet you, Agent Miller and Sergeant Durick. I am special Agent Robert Murphy, and the members of my unit will introduce themselves. Trudy, would you like to begin the introductions?"

"Hi, my name is Trudy Bell. My job is to be present at autopsies to make sure everything is recorded correctly for legal reasons. I am also the public information officer. I have been with the BAU for about twelve years."

"My name is Clark Daniels, and I am a forensic psychologist. I have been with the unit for about seven years."

My name is Mark Wilson, and I am a forensic investigator specializing in tracking of phone calls and internet data. I have been with the unit fourteen years."

Special Agent Murphy is requesting that we all take a seat around the table so that we can get started.

After a long period of time going over reports, watching films, and looking at photographs, it is nearing nine o'clock. It has been a very informative and productive meeting.

Agent Murphy has just stood up from his seat. "Sergeant Durick and Agent Miller, my team will be working late into the night. You are free to go home and get some rest; it will be a busy day tomorrow."

He requests that I arrange a temporary meeting space for him and his unit at the State Police headquarters building where they will be accessing resources to complete the investigation through the Indianapolis field office and the Chicago FBI buildings.

As Agent Miller's team and the rest of us stand up to leave, we all shake hands, and we thank them again for coming.

I return to the entryway door, stop to turn in my visitor's badge, and walk to my car. As I buckle up, I plan the rest of my night. A shower and straight to bed is a must for me. It's going to be a short night and a long day tomorrow.

Chapter Sixteen - Small Thread of Hope

It is beginning to get dark in here, and I am becoming more and more depressed as time goes by. He will be returning to the building in a few days, so I only have a short time to convince the woman who roams these halls that she can trust me. I must make her understand that I need to get out of here to make it possible to get help - not just for me but for her and all of the other poor women in this building who have been abducted and held against their will. I must find a way to gain her trust.

I know that she is afraid, and that is why she looks over her shoulder before she gives me something to eat or drink. I am sure that she has probably thought about all the consequences that she would have to face if she were to get caught helping me. So how am I going to get through to her?

As I sit up on the edge of my bed, I can see a faint hint of light. It appears to be slowly getting a little brighter, and faint shadows are starting to appear in the hallway. They seem to shift up and down as though they are dancing on the wall as the light becomes brighter. It is her, holding the oil lamp and walking toward my cell. "Thank you God!"

She is reaching up and placing the handle of the lamp over a nail on the wall and turning to unlock my cell door. As she is walking toward me, she reaches into her apron pocket and pulls out a white cloth and a piece of rope.

The door to my cell is standing open, and I can't help but think that I could quickly push her backward and try to run through the open door. But would she understand that I would be leaving to try to get help for all of us, or would she feel betrayed? God, I am not sure if I should take this chance. My uncertainty makes it too late to try.

She is reaching over and binding my wrists together with the rope and is placing the cloth over my eyes and tying it behind my head. If she is going to let me walk in the hall with her, doesn't she understand that I need to see where these hallways lead? Or maybe she is preparing me to face another nightmare! "Please dear God, she is the only hope that I have!"

I can feel her hand touching mine and grasping it as she pulls me up on my feet. She moves my hand and places it on top of her arm, and we begin to walk forward. I am feeling very unsteady on my feet and unsure of myself. I have to depend on her to guide me. I can feel the cool cement floor on my feet and hear her taking the lamp off the nail. I can only hope that she is leading me to an exit. But why did she have to blindfold me?

I am taking small steps and feeling very confused and scared. "Please, God, don't let her take me to a room to be abused like those other women who were in his coming attractions. He tortured Maggie, and she was missing all of her fingertips." Just the thought of this is making me feel very anxious, and my heart is beginning to pound. It is not hot in here, but I can feel the perspiration as it seeps through the pores of my skin, leaving me feeling clammy. The muscles in my body are beginning to tense up and ache more and more with each unsure step I take.

At least twenty minutes must have passed by, and we have taken many steps and turns in several different directions. She is taking my arm and placing it down by my side and removing her hand from me. What is she doing? "Please, where are you? Don't just leave me standing here alone!"

I can hear a loud noise directly in front of me. It sounds like a steel door sliding, and I can feel her placing her hands around my ankle and trying to lift up my foot and place it in front of me. As I set my foot down, I can feel that the surface of the floor has changed. She grabs my hand and pulls me forward and then releases my hand. I jump at the sound of a loud bang behind me that sounds as though a large, heavy door had been slammed shut, and I can feel movement that is throwing me off balance. "Are you here with me?"

She doesn't answer, but I can hear a grinding and knocking noise as the movement continues. Very quickly it all stops, and I hear the door opening again. I feel her placing her hands on my shoulders and turning me around. She is lifting up my foot again and placing it back down then pulling me forward. I can feel a soft cushion on my feet as though I am standing on carpeting. We begin walking again, and she guides me toward the right, then stops and releases my hand.

She pulls on the cloth at the back of my head as she unties the knot and then removes it from my eyes and unwinds the rope from my wrists. I stand here in shock and total disbelief at what I am seeing. This isn't a cell; it's an actual bedroom! She is pushing me toward the bed and pointing for me to sit down. The painted walls are very bare and stark, but the bed is covered with real sheets. The dresser is bare except for a small hairbrush sitting on the top. There are no mirrors, decorations, or pictures anywhere in the room. The closet has no door, and I can see that there are three or four old dresses hanging on hooks.

She walks toward the closet and bends over to pick up her basket of dolls. As she is walking back toward me, she is holding the basket out for me to take from her. Oh God, she has glued my hair that she chopped off onto the heads of each and every one of these dolls! She walks to the dresser, picks up her hairbrush, and turns around to walk back and hand it to me. I reach into the basket and pick up one of the dolls and carefully brush the doll's hair. She gently pulls it out of my hands and holds it to her chest, embracing it as though it is a real child. I pick up each doll and brush its hair and then place each one back into her basket, pulling the blanket up to partially cover them.

I can't imagine what this woman has gone through in her lifetime, and I can't even begin to understand why she has not tried to leave this place, especially with him being away from the building.

After reaching over to remove the basket of dolls from my lap, she places the doll she was cradling in her arms back into the basket and walks over to put them back on the closet floor. Returning to me, she begins to tie my wrists as before. "Please don't cover my eyes. You can trust me. I will help you take care of your beautiful dolls."

She stuffs the cloth back into her apron pocket and is helping me up off the bed, holding my arm as we walk to the door. We turn to the left, but as I glance to the right, I can see a beautifully decorated room at the end of a long hallway. I catch a glimpse of a very impressive long, gold curtain and a floor-to-ceiling bookcase filled with books. We proceed to walk about ten feet, and there is an old, rusted door that she is pulling open. It is a very decrepit and spooky-looking elevator. After stepping inside, she closes the door and pushes a button. I know that we have passed at least three floors on the way down and can once again hear the screeching and banging noises.

We have come to a stop, and she is pulling the door open. She grabs an oil lamp that was sitting on the floor next to the door, and we begin to walk down a dark corridor, making a turn to the right and then walking for quite a long distance before making a left turn. As we reach my cell door, she unties my hands and lightly pushes me into my room and locks the door. "Thank you for showing me your dolls and for trusting me to walk with you without wearing a blindfold. Please think about helping me to escape from this building."

It is once again becoming very dark in here as she walks away with the lamp. When I reach my bed after feeling my way in the dark, I lie down to rest and think. She has her own room upstairs, as depressing as it is, but the room down the hall looked very elaborate. Has she tried to get out of here and been severely punished for doing so? Her face is badly scarred, and she is missing part of her tongue. How could she want to stay here? I know that she does his dirty-work for him before he sexually brutalizes women and probably cleans and cooks for him, but why was she able to earn the right to roam around? Is he still sexually molesting her? Or is her mind just too far gone after all the horrible things she has been through to even care anymore?

"Dear God, I am tired and depressed. Please help me and the rest of these women. Please stop him somehow from abducting the woman he is searching for now. And God, even though I am detained in a horrible situation, I am still very thankful to be alive! Amen."

Chapter Seventeen - Meeting at Headquarters

"Good Morning, Nancy. Just to give you a heads up, the BAU that was called in on the Margaret Lewis case will be using our large conference room as a temporary office space starting this morning. I am going to ask the officers and the other office personnel to assist me in getting the room set up for them as quickly as possible. They will probably be arriving here soon."

"Sergeant Durick, is there anything that I can do to help?"

"If you could take a minute to get some coffee and pitchers of water ready, that would be great. I'm sure that they will be asking all of us to assist them in some way during their stay here."

"No problem, sir."

After requesting some help from the staff, we are all busy trying to get the room setup completed. We have several flip charts, pens, and tablets, and the access number to the wireless internet has been written on the chalkboard. Several staff members are now carrying in a large screen and projector, two laptop computers, and more chairs. I have placed a map of the U.S. on the corkboard that is attached to the west wall, and the phones in the room will give them access to four incoming and outgoing lines for conference calling if needed. There are plenty of chairs around the table now to accommodate quite a few people. I believe we are ready.

"Thank you everyone for your help. I will call you if there is anything else that the BAU may need or require."

As the office staff is leaving the room, the patrol and desk officers have all taken a seat around the table. I am standing next to the phone as it begins to ring.

"Yes, Nancy?"

"Sergeant Durick, the unit has just arrived."

"Thanks, Nancy. I will be right there."

As I walk out of the conference room and down the hall, I can see them all standing in the lobby.

"Good morning Special Agent Murphy and Agents Bell, Daniels and Wilson. If you will all follow me, I will show you to the conference room. The patrol and desk officers are already present per your request. Nancy has made coffee, and there are glasses on the table for any of you that would like ice water."

As we all are taking a seat, agent Murphy begins. "My team and I worked late into the night, and there are still many loopholes and unanswered questions in this case. Agent Wilson has completed a DVD containing the photos of the deceased victim, Margaret Lewis, and five other women that are in some way linked to this homicide. I will give you a short presentation now and a more detailed report at this afternoon's meeting. Agent Wilson, would you go ahead and put the DVD in the computer, and I will continue speaking as you present the slides."

The door opens, and Agent Murphy greets the men as they enter the room. "Good morning Agents Miller and Greene. Have a seat; we are just getting started.

"This first slide is a picture of our deceased victim, Margaret Lewis. She was abducted out of Chicago, Illinois, several months ago from the parking lot of a department store. We have requested that the officers who have been working on this case attend our meeting this afternoon and bring in all of their files and records that are pertinent to this investigation. According to the National Missing Persons Database the deceased was a white female, thirty-one years old, and has been missing since April twenty-ninth of this year. She was five foot four and a half inches tall, weighed one hundred ten pounds four ounces, with brown hair and brown eyes. Her body was found in a shallow grave at the Country Church Cemetery on Radcliff Road here in Indiana. She was buried, while still alive, in the same grave as a gentleman by the name of Jason Pratt. She died from suffocation. Agent Miller from the CSI will be showing his slides and going over her autopsy reports in much greater detail with all of you later.

"This second slide is Shelby Grey. She is believed to have been abducted from the parking lot at a night spot called the Five Mile Roundup in Nashville, Tennessee, on June twenty-ninth of this year. Her prints were found on the deceased victim's body during the autopsy. Shelby is also white, five foot two inches tall, one hundred and five pounds, with blonde hair and blue eyes. We spoke to Detective Morse and Deputy Ron Taylor from the County Sheriff's office in Nashville last evening, and one of Sergeant Durick's officers is in flight as we speak to pick up the reports from their office. When speaking with Detective Morse, who was assigned her case, he advised me that a picture of her naked body restrained to a bed was found on her cell phone. There was also a DVD of Shelby Grey that was sent to her mother, Peggy Grey, postmarked from Kentucky. The DVD, according to Detective Morse, showed that Shelby Grey was standing naked next to a graveside with a shovel in her hand. We will be reviewing their reports and the DVD during this afternoon's meeting."

"Agent Wilson, could you please proceed to the next slide.

"Agents Miller and Greene were present and assisted with the autopsy of Margaret Lewis that was overseen and conducted by Dr. Daniel Pash, the Medical Examiner, and Coroner Gustafson. This is a picture of the X-ray that was taken of Margaret Lewis's large intestine. You can see here the four dark spots that appear on this image. After cutting open the intestine, four fingertips were found inside and removed from her organ. The DNA reports on the bone fragments and tissue that were found came back confirming that the fingertips were those of four other women.

"The next slides are those of four other women who are also still missing. Two of these women are considered to be cold cases. Every lead was followed up and then just came to a stop because of lack of clues and evidence. We have requested that all of the evidence from each location on these four cases be electronically transmitted to us by noon today by their local authorities. We will be downloading and carefully going over all these reports at our meeting this afternoon.

"The slide that Agent Wilson has just pulled up is a picture of a white female by the name of Mary Gibbs. She was assumed to have been abducted from a bike trail on May 29, 2012, in Cedar Falls, Iowa. She was a student at a local college and was only eighteen years old. She was five foot tall, weighed one hundred and two pounds, blonde hair and blue eyes. She is one of the two cold cases that I previously mentioned.

"This slide is a picture of Patsy Harkness, white female, believed to have been abducted from a back parking lot of a bar called Ray's Sports Bar and Grille in Davenport, Iowa. She has been missing since August 29, 2013. She is twenty-two years old. Her height is five foot three inches; weight is one hundred one pounds, blonde hair and blue eyes. There is an ongoing investigation on her, but no new leads until now.

"Our next missing victim is Jody Taylor. She is a white female believed to have been abducted while taking her evening walk on a rural road in Hazel Green, Wisconsin. She is twenty-five years old, five foot two inches, one hundred nine pounds, light brown hair, blue eyes. Her abduction took place on October 29, 2013. There was a picture of her lying naked in a wooded area found on her cell phone. The phone was found in the timber during a search, but there was no trace of her body. This case is still being investigated.

"Our last slide is Carolyn Nickerson. Carolyn is a white female, twenty-six years old, height five foot three and a half inches, weight one hundred eleven pounds, auburn colored hair, and green eyes. She was reported to have been abducted while jogging on the evening of June 29, 2012, from a small park in Portage, Indiana, near a wooded area. Her case was investigated heavily, but there was no evidence found that could confirm her abduction. This case has been considered a cold file.

"Well, officers and agents, as I mentioned earlier, we are waiting for police and autopsy reports to come in from other agencies, and I hope to be able to go over all of these cases this afternoon in greater detail. I'm sure you all have noticed that each of these women went missing on the twenty-ninth day of different months. We will dismiss for an hour for lunch, and I will see you all back here at one o'clock. We hope to be far enough along with our investigation by five p.m. to be able to have Agent Bell schedule a news conference with the press and the reporters from all the news stations at seven p.m. Please do not discuss any of this information with anybody outside of this room."

Chapter Eighteen - Inflicting Fear and Pain

As I look down at this naked young woman who is tied to the bed of my truck, I am feeling no remorse. I am, however, anxious to relieve my sexual needs and fulfill my fantasies soon! Why would this young girl, walking alone to her car late at night, assume that she would be exempt from the horrors of this world? She was completely in her own little shallow mental space, absorbed in her cell phone, as though her night was just going to be a typical one. She either let down her guard or she is just totally oblivious to the terrors that can exist in the darkness. She's stupid - women are all so stupid!

I pull myself up into the cab and begin to drive and search for a side road to travel on, one that's away from any traffic and is less of a risk of being caught. By the time the drug that I forcefully injected into her neck begins to wear off, I know that I can find a safe, secluded area to take my clothes off and lay my body on top of hers, unleashing all of these inner sexual and mental desires that I am carrying inside of me.

I think I will turn on a dim light and look at my prized possession on the computer screen. She is still lying there quietly, with her legs and arms spread widely apart, tied to the bed posts. She looks very young and innocent: she's short and petite with pretty blonde hair. She appears to be so childlike. I have not yet checked out her driver's license to see how old she actually is.

I am going to keep driving to allow time for the drug to wear off and make sure that we are miles away from the abduction site. She is very small built, and it will take quite a while for her to regain consciousness. I want this one to be fully aware of what I am doing to her body so that I can see the pain and fear in her eyes. Just the thought of this excites me mentally and sexually!

There have not been any cars pass by, so I know this is not a heavily traveled road. Other than the light from the moon, it's pretty dark out here. Glancing at her again on my computer screen, I can see that she is still passed out from the drug. I am going to continue to drive.

Several hours have passed by, but I think I will still try to drive through a few more small towns before pulling over to get something to eat. If this young girl still happened to live with

119

her parents, there is a chance they will alert the cops upon her not returning home. I will continue to stay on a less-traveled, two lane road for a while just to be on the safe side.

The small, green road sign said twelve miles until I reach the next town. Hopefully I can find a restaurant there so I can grab a bite to eat. These small towns usually only have one cop, two at the most, on duty at this time of night, so I can rest a little, eat, and hit the road again. I gagged her mouth, and the truck is soundproof, so if she wakes up while I am eating, she will not be heard by anyone.

All right, the sign says population nine hundred. I wonder if this place is big enough for a restaurant. As I'm driving slowly through town, I'm not seeing anything. Wait a minute, there is a little mom and pop place to the right on the edge of town. There are a few cars in the parking lot, so I think I will pull off to the left side, away from the street light.

It feels good to get out and stretch my legs. As I'm walking in the doorway, I see eight stools at the counter and five tables. The furniture is very old, and the waitress looks just about as worn out as the place does. After I sit down at one of the stools, she approaches me, carrying a pot of coffee.

"Would you like some coffee, sir?"

"Yes thanks, and could I also order a cheeseburger with the works?"

As she places the ticket through the order window, the door opens. I turn, and an officer is walking toward me.

"Good evening, officer."

"Good evening, nice quiet night."

"Yep, I thought I would grab a quick bite to eat. Just passing through, moving my sister's furniture. She finally gave in and is moving back to her home town."

"Yes, I saw a truck outside with Georgia plates."

"Yes sir, small truck. She didn't have a whole lot. It's hard to make it on your own anymore, so she decided to move closer to family."

The waitress sets my cheeseburger down in front of me, and I pick it up and begin to eat. The officer is sitting at the counter to my right, sipping on his coffee and having a conversation with the waitress.

"Good food. Do you have my bill?"

She sets the bill on the counter, and I take the money out of my wallet.

"Here you go, Miss. Keep the change."

The officer glances over. "You have a safe trip to Georgia."

"Thanks sir, you have a good night."

Walking out the door and across the lot, I can't help but think that the cop is just about as stupid as women. Although, even if he had run my plate number, he wouldn't have found anything.

As I pull out of the lot and back onto the road, I decide that I will continue to drive on this two lane road and maybe later catch the interstate. I should probably turn on a dim light and check on my passenger. As I look at my computer screen, I can see that she is beginning to move her head around. I reach down and turn on the speaker. "Hey little missy, why were you out all alone at night in the dark? Don't you know that there are men like me out there looking for a young piece of ass? Lights out now, little one. Try to relax and get some rest!"

I think I will turn off this road onto the interstate up ahead. I have the feeling that it will be safer traveling on the interstate for a while and then switching back to a two lane to get to where I want to be.

I am anxious to get my penis into that nice little thing, but I don't want to get caught after getting away with it all these years. It has been way too much fun to have to give it up! I will just keep driving until I feel safe. The wait will just make it that much more exciting and stimulating.

Chapter Nineteen - Afternoon Meeting

All of the officers, CSI Agents Miller and Greene, and I have taken our seats around the table in the conference room. Special Agent Murphy and Agents Bell, Daniels, and Wilson are now entering the room and taking the empty seats at the table.

Special Agent Murphy begins the meeting as he walks over to the chalk board. "Well, ladies and gentlemen, we definitely have our work cut out for us this afternoon. We will be going over the reports that were sent in from other agencies, some specifics on the homicide of Margaret Lewis, and some disturbing discoveries and reports that were pulled from the National Missing Persons Database."

With a report in his hand, Agent Murphy moves to the map of the United States and begins to place colored pushpins into eight different states on the map. "Officers and Agents, according to the reports that I had Sergeant Durick's office staff working on all morning, we have a total of about twenty to thirty missing women, over an eight state area, that have similar evidence in each case. We have requested that more information on each case be forwarded to the FBI office in Chicago. We are asking their agents to assist us in determining if this could be one individual who has committed all of these abductions and, in some of these cases, homicides. The crimes took place over an extended period of time.

"The yellow pins that I have placed on the map indicate where bodies of women that were listed on the missing persons list have been found. They were all badly sexually and physically abused. Some of these women were buried in shallow gravesites in various locations, others in dense wooded areas, and some in rural fields. In each of these cases, a small stem of artificial flowers was found at the location of each body. After reading the report from Agent Miller, we noticed that his evidence report on Margaret Lewis stated that there was a stem of purple violets found buried with her body.

"Later today Agent Daniels will be working with several forensic psychologists from the bureau in Chicago to gather complete reports on these particular women and to compare the evidence and their autopsy reports. They will also be checking their abduction dates and how long it was before the bodies were discovered.

We need to know how long these women were in captivity before they died.

"The red pins on this map represent women who have been missing for five years or longer, and the blue pins are for the women who have been missing from two to five years. The green pins represent all of the women who have been reported missing this year including Shelby Grey, who was most recently reported missing.

"Agent Wilson, let's go over all the slides and information from this morning again. We all need to take notes as we go."

After several hours Agent Murphy says, "I think, at this point, we will take a fifteen minute break. During this time feel free to discuss this information among yourselves. I will have a period of time prior to the end of the meeting to answer all of your questions."

As we all get up to stretch our legs and take a bathroom break, Agent Murphy is talking to Agent Bell. I would imagine they are discussing a plan to get a report ready for the press release that is scheduled for this evening.

Agent Murphy is a tall man, quite distinguished looking, and very large and muscular. He has probably seen just about everything in his twenty-plus years at the BAU. He is all business and definitely knows what he is doing. With everyone working as a team, I have no doubt that he will find this murderer and get him off the streets.

"Ladies and gentlemen, please take your seats, and we will get this meeting underway. During our short break, I was handed an updated report on the similarities of the missing women. We are looking at possibly thirty-three cases that could be linked together in some way. At this point we will be reaching out for assistance from FBI field offices and many police headquarters across eight different states.

"All of the thirty-three missing women were abducted in the evening. They were all between the ages of eighteen and thirty-three, all very close in height and weight, but with different hair color. Each of them was known to be alone when the abduction took place, and up until this time, there have not been any witnesses that have come forward. In the Margaret Lewis case, we feel that the other five women could possibly still be alive and held somewhere against their will.

"Agent Wilson, would you pull up the picture that was found on Shelby Grey's cell phone? If you look closely, you can see that she appears to be unconscious and is strapped to a bed, naked. Looking closely, I see no bruising on her body. This picture and the cell phone need to be sent over to the crime scene lab to be analyzed. Agent Wilson will be present to assist them while they go through all of the incoming and outgoing calls, messages, and other pictures. Detective Morse from the County Sheriff's Department in Nashville went through her phone, but we need to check all of the contacts in the phone, along with the other items that I mentioned, again. We need to see if we can determine, from the wall behind her, where this picture was taken.

"Now Agent Wilson, could you put in the DVD that was mailed from Kentucky to Shelby Grey's mother, Ann Grey? This footage shows Shelby, naked, holding a shovel and digging a grave. Next we see her sitting next to Margaret Lewis, who is lying in the shallow grave. You can see by looking at the recording that both Shelby and Margaret are crying. The lab will be able to digitally expand this shot to confirm that Margaret Lewis was still alive while lying in the shallow grave. Next the footage shows Shelby getting on top of a tombstone to sit. The fear in her face pretty much says that she was being forced by somebody to do this. All of this needs to be checked by the experts at the lab. If the abductor keeps Shelby two months before killing her, like he did with Margaret Lewis, we might have a chance to save her.

"The bone fragments and tissue samples that were removed from Margaret Lewis's large intestine were examined by Agent Miller and Agent Greene. They are known to belong to Mary Gibbs, Patsy Harkness, Jody Taylor, and Carolyn Nickerson as we said this morning. The next of kin of all these women have been notified, as well as Mrs. Peggy Grey.

"We are asking that all of you heavily patrol parks, department store parking lots, bike paths, and anyplace else where somebody could possibly abduct women. Please do not discuss any details of this case with anyone, including your family. We are going to dismiss this meeting for today to allow us time to prepare for the news conference tonight. Thank you all for your assistance. Are there any questions at this time?"

There is silence in the room until Agent Murphy continues. "No questions? Sergeant Durick, Agent Miller, and Agent Greene, I would like you to be present at the press conference here tonight at 7:00 p.m. Agent Trudy Bell will be speaking to the press and news reporters on behalf of the BAU."

Chapter Twenty - My Locket - My Hope

As I lie here in the dark, I feel a deep loss of hope and completely isolated from all of the things I love the most in my life. "I know you are with me God, but I am in desperate fear for my life and the lives of all of the other women who are being raped and tortured in this place. I know this man is very mentally sick, but I can't fight off the hatred that I am carrying in my heart. I know that you are forgiving of the sins that people commit, but I am struggling to forget the pain that he has inflicted upon me and so many others. Please hear my prayers, and help me to understand the path that you have laid out for me to follow. Amen."

It is very quiet, and I can feel my heart pounding. I know that I might have only one more day, if that, to win the trust of this woman who roams the halls. He will be returning soon, and because I upset him prior to his leaving the building, I am sure he is ready to show me how repugnant, heartless, and cruel he is. "Please God, have her return to my cell. Time is running out!

"The locket that you gave me, Daddy, has always made me feel as though you are with me and that it is a part of you. Several times the woman has lifted it off my chest and held it in her hand. I know that the material things in life have no real value and that you will always remain in my heart with or without it. Would you forgive me if I offer it to this woman to try to show her I can be trusted?"

I can hear someone unlocking the door! I quickly roll over but can barely see who is entering my room. It's her! Why is she not using an oil- lamp? She is reaching down, taking my hand to pull me up. She begins to cross my hands and tie them tightly in front of me and then pulls me up on my feet. She leads me through the doorway of my cell, turns to the left, and proceeds to walk me down the hallway.

The hallways are dark and quiet as we continue to walk and make turns leading to other hallways. We have reached the elevator, and she is sliding the door back to open it. After stepping into the elevator and hearing the door screech shut, I hear the grinding sounds and feel the movement. I can hear her breathing heavily in this dark space. I can only pray that she is taking me to an exit and will release me. But if she is going to let me go, why would she tie my hands together so tightly?

The elevator has stopped, and as the door opens we step out onto the carpeted area. Does she want me to brush the hair on her dolls again? She is not stopping at the room she took me to before. Instead, she continues to walk with me toward the light at the end of the hallway.

I must pay close attention to every detail. As we enter through the open doorway, I am completely speechless! The room is beyond elegant, and the furniture and décor are magnificent! I see shelves from the floor to the high ceiling that are completely filled with books. There is also a large desk with a stained glass lamp on it along with a computer, a printer and some neatly stacked papers.

We are leaving that room and are soon standing in a huge den filled with the most beautiful furniture that I have ever seen. There are expensive pieces of art on the walls and a large fireplace, but I see no mirrors or any family pictures.

We continue through more rooms and pass by many closed doors and are now going down a flight of steps to another completely furnished level of rooms. As we walk past an open door to the right, I can see a huge master bedroom with a sitting area, a large bed with posts that go from the bed to the ceiling, dressers, and another fireplace but again, no mirrors.

She is now leading me down another winding staircase to a third level of living space that contains a kitchen area, a sunroom filled with plants and furniture, and a living room with more art pieces, expensive stained glass lamps, and beautiful furniture.

From the front window of the living room I can see a row of lampposts and, with the light reflecting from them, part of a circular driveway with flowers surrounding the whole area. In the distance there are many faint lights, as though this beautiful place sits in a remote area away from everyone and everything.

She is beginning to lead me back the way we came, and as we pass through the kitchen she picks up a cluster of red grapes from a beautiful glass bowl that sits on the kitchen table and then reaches into the refrigerator for a bottle of water. She places the items in her apron pocket. We continue back to the staircase and up the steps to the second level, through the rooms, and back up the last flight of steps until we reach the level where we started.

As we pass through the den and into the room with the desk and bookshelves, she pauses and gazes at a piece of artwork hanging on the wall. It has two black circles joined together and one black circle standing alone. Red blood-like splatters cover the whole painting. It almost looks as though the paint is dripping off the canvas.

We are now proceeding down the hallway toward the elevator. She turns left into the room where I combed her dolls' hair. Still holding my arm, she reaches into the dresser and pulls out a badly blood-stained gown, like one would wear in a hospital, and then walks me back to the door and down the hall to the elevator. She slides the door open, and we are once again standing in the dark on the spooky, noisy elevator. When we reach the bottom floor she leads me by my arm off the elevator, back down the hallways, and to my cell. Once there, she guides me to the bed, lifts up the mattress, and shoves the gown under it then lightly pushes me down to a sitting position. She removes the ropes from my wrists and reaches into her apron pocket to give me the grapes and water before turning to leave.

"Please wait, I have something for you!"

She turns back around as I reach up to take the locket from my neck. "I would like you to have this, and I would like you to think about helping me. Please, at least think about it!"

She holds the necklace in her hand, places her hand on top of my head, then walks away and locks the cell door behind her.

I touch my neck and chest, and I realize that I am crying. I have worn that necklace since the day my dad gave it to me. He is gone, and I miss him so much, and now the gift that he gave me is also gone. "Please Dad, I hope you understand why I gave up the gift that you gave me, and God, please let this small sacrifice that I have made be my way out of here."

I am lying back down, and though I feel exhausted, I can't shut my mind off in order to get some rest. How could someone have a house with all of those beautiful things and be so hateful inside? I don't understand how there could be that much beauty in those front three stories of this place and the back three stories hold such a horrifying feeling of fear and death. Why were there no mirrors or family pictures anywhere? Why did she feel she had to show me that part of this place? Would going through that part of the house be my only way out of here because all the other exits are gated and locked? Why did she hide that blood-stained gown under my mattress? I don't understand. There are so many mixed signs!

"Dear God, Mister will probably be returning tomorrow, and I know that he will torture me in some way. If this happens, give me the strength that I will need to survive, and don't let him take possession of my soul. When he returns, please let it be without another victim in his possession."

Chapter Twenty-One - Deathly Pleasure

I have traveled countless miles and am anxious to satisfy my sexual needs, but maybe getting one more state away from the abduction site would be in my best interest.

I can see her on the computer screen. She is struggling to try to free herself from the bed, but it is a task that she will not accomplish because I have restrained her wrists and ankles securely.

"Miss Ashley, I know you can hear me over the speaker back there. Are you ready to be brutally raped? I know I am more than ready to unload my sexual needs! You are only seventeen years old; didn't your mother ever teach you to watch out for men like me in the dark? I might pull this truck over soon; it looks like you are struggling to breathe with that rag I tied around your mouth. I am sure you're going to enjoy it. I am very good at what I do. I have had a lot of practice. Hang in there for a little longer, and don't wet the bed. I will use a catheter on you. I like to be able to see you and touch you when I do this! Settle down, or you are going to wear yourself out! Breaker one – over and out!"

I cannot breathe! My asthma is causing me to feel like I am going to pass out, and I am unable to get enough oxygen with this rag restricting the amount of air getting into my lungs. My anxiety is not helping much either. I am so afraid right now that my chest is rising up and down, and my heart feels like it could jump out of my chest. I did not see this man's face. I felt a sharp pain in my neck and could feel something digging deeply into the skin on my face and throat, and I could feel myself going down. I need my inhaler, or I am not going to make it. The tears are streaming out of my eyes and down my cheeks. I feel like I am going to vomit! "How and why, God, is this happening?" I need to concentrate on breathing in deeply through my nose and slowly releasing the air as best I can through my mouth. I am very light-headed, and I feel like I'm spinning around in circles.

"Miss Ashley, I am pulling off the road up ahead. Are you ready for me? I was going to wait to get you to the building, but I can't bring myself to wait any longer! Over and out!"

There is a place nearby where I can pull right into a cornfield and not be seen by anyone. I could be taking a slight chance, but at this point I can't wait any longer to relieve myself. I am going to turn a dim light back on so I can see to insert a catheter inside her.

I have stopped now and am getting down out of the cab. I need to take a piss before getting in the back of the truck with her. This one could be a quickie, just to relieve myself, and then when I get her back to the building, I can work her over good. I am pulling down the ramp, walking up into the truck, and pulling the doors closed behind me.

"Well, Miss Ashley, let's take that rag off of your mouth. If you try to scream you will be so sorry! Why are you breathing so hard? Is it because you are looking forward to this?"

"Mister, I need my inhaler. I am struggling to breathe!"

"Lift up your mid-section, so I can slide this pan under you to catch the urine. Now I just need to spread you apart and place this catheter inside you... ah, there it comes. Now lift up so I can get this pan back out from under you. I am going to wipe you and play with you for a few minutes."

"Oh God, please don't do this to me! You are hurting me! I can't breathe! Please get me my inhaler!"

"You don't need an inhaler; I am going to be doing all of the work. Just lie there and enjoy it!"

He is wearing a mask so that I can't see his face, and his hands are covered with surgical gloves. Now he is taking off his clothes and feeling and playing with himself. He has put on a condom and is swinging his leg over me and is straddling me on the bed like he is mounting a horse. I am feeling like I could faint! I can feel him penetrating deep inside of me, and I am gasping for air. He is thrusting himself back and forth in me faster and faster. I am in pain and can't breathe! I can feel myself drifting away.

"Miss Ashley, wake up! Do you hear me? Wake up!"

She is not breathing, and I cannot feel a pulse in her neck. When I lift her eyelids, there is no eye movement. She is dead! I need to get dressed and get the hell out of this field! I can get rid of her body when I get back. I will bury her in the timber behind the building.

I'm back up in the cab and starting to back out of the field. I know that I will have to make sure there are no cars coming before I pull completely out of the field and then out onto the road.

At least I was able to satisfy my needs, but now I will have to travel straight through to get back and get rid of her body before she starts to decompose and stink up my trunk. I should be back before daylight. I can get her buried and then rest for a while. I still have to settle up with Miss Shelby. She will lose all the faith she thinks she has in God by the time I'm finished with her.

I have reached my destination. I will pull into the timber behind the building, and maybe I will just pull her body out of the truck and onto the ground and bury her later. There is never anybody near this place anyway because of its location. I ditched her phone after taking a picture of her with it and kept her license, so I will just bury her purse with her. I do feel cheated after traveling all of those miles and getting only one quick piece of ass. It doesn't seem like it was worth my time and effort.

Maybe I will need to give Shelby another good sexual workout. This time I know I can break her spirit. She humiliated me by laughing at me before I left the building. She won't be laughing by the time I'm finished with her. I think that I'll just take a quick walk past her room. It will give her something more to pray about.

"Miss Shelby, did you miss me? Aren't you glad that I am back?"

I hear the cruel and evil sound of his laugh as he walks away from my cell door. "Dear God, I have given up hope of being able to leave this building. Now I can only ask that you stand by my side and continue to protect me from death and the demons that exist within him. Amen."

Chapter Twenty-Two - News Conference and Updates

"Good evening, Nancy. Thank you for your prompt assistance in getting all of the reporters and media notified about our news conference this evening. I am sure they will all be arriving within an hour. Agent Bell, our public information officer, will be speaking on behalf of the BAU. Have the other agents and Sergeant Durick arrived yet?"

"Yes sir, they are all waiting in the conference room."

"We have about an hour to go over some new information that I received, and Agent Bell can fill us in on her statement that she has prepared. Can you buzz us when the reporters arrive?"

"Yes sir, will do."

As I walk into the conference room, I can see that everyone is present. Agent Murphy says, "Agent Bell, could you stand and fill us all in on the report that you have prepared for the conference?"

"Yes, Agent Murphy. I will be giving an update on the Margaret Lewis case but will be divulging only brief facts at this time. The news media sometimes have a tendency to exaggerate what they report to the public, and that can hurt the case rather than help it. I will be stressing to them the importance of getting the message across to all women that there is a chance that the predator could still be located in this area. We have found that being as brief as possible is important until more facts are known about the case."

"Thank you, Agent Bell. We all realize that with the cyber world being what it is today, news can travel fast.

"I spoke to an FBI Agent out of the Chicago location about an hour ago. His team is aggressively researching the abduction dates and locations. With thirty-three possible victims, it will take several days working long hours to come up with the information that we need.

"Also, Agent Daniels will be working over at the Chicago FBI building with a team of forensic psychologists over the next few days to try to determine if these cases are similar enough to tie them down to one suspect. With the evidence that we have at this time, they will hopefully be able to tell us what makes this guy tick."

The phone is buzzing. "Agent Murphy speaking."

"Agent Murphy, the media and the reporters have all arrived."

"Thanks Nancy. We will be there in just a few minutes."

"Well, everyone, it is time for the news conference. I will be doing the introductions, and then Agent Bell will be speaking. Shall we all proceed to the lobby?"

We walk down the hall toward the lobby where the reporters have already started to film and take pictures.

"Good evening, ladies and gentlemen. I would appreciate it if you could all back up a little bit with your equipment to allow us more room. I am also requesting that you hold your questions until after our public information officer is finished speaking.

"I am Special Agent Robert Murphy from the Behavioral Analysis Unit out of the FBI Headquarters in Washington, D.C. I would like to introduce you to the rest of my team members and others that are assisting us in this investigation. If you could please step forward as I call your name: Agent Clark Daniels, our forensic psychologist; Agent Mark Wilson, our forensic investigator; and Agent Trudy Bell, who is our public information officer and will be speaking tonight on behalf of our team. To my left I would like to introduce Agent Miller and Agent Greene from the CSI and Sergeant Durick who is representing this facility. Agent Bell, could you please proceed with your report?"

"Ladies and gentlemen, our team has been called in on a homicide case that occurred in Indiana, in a small cemetery off of Radcliff Road. The victim's name is Margaret Lewis from Chicago, Illinois. Her body was found buried in a shallow grave above a deceased man named Jason Pratt who was buried in that same plot. After an autopsy was performed by a medical examiner, it is known that street drugs were in her body, and she was buried alive and died of suffocation from the dirt that was covering her body. The medical examiner also discovered bone fragments in her large intestine. These fragments, through DNA testing, were found to be from four other women whose names are not being released at this time. There was a set of fingerprints lifted from the deceased victim's body, and through testing we were able to match the prints to that of a Shelby Grey from Nashville, Tennessee. Shelby was abducted on June 29, 2014, and was placed on the National Missing Persons Database.

"At this time we are searching for a sexual predator as well as a murder suspect. We would like to emphasize again that all women need to be extremely cautious and not be out unaccompanied in the evening hours. We are asking that if anyone has any information on this case to report it to the Indiana State Patrol Headquarters immediately.

"I can answer a few questions at this time. Yes sir, what is your question?"

"Agent Bell, are we to assume that Margaret Lewis was sexually molested?"

"Yes sir, that is correct, but no DNA was present. Yes sir, what is your question?"

"Do you think that the other women are still alive and that he has them held somewhere in Indiana?"

"We are hoping, at this point in time, that they are still alive and that he might have them held somewhere against their will, but the location of his site could be in this state or possibly another state. Yes ma'am. What is your question?"

"How old are the women who have been mentioned, and are they all from the Chicago area?"

"They range from eighteen to thirty-two years of age, but I am unable to answer the second part of your question at this time. Yes sir?"

"Do you have any suspects in this case?"

"No sir, we don't. Ladies and gentlemen, I will be unable to answer any more questions. We will keep you updated after having more time to investigate this homicide. Thank you and have a good evening."

Agent Murphy is walking back down the hall to the conference room, and the other agents are following behind him. I am going to try to clear these reporters out of here!

"Sergeant Durick, could you answer a few more questions for us?"

"No sir, I can't. I will have to ask you all to start clearing your equipment out of the lobby."

Now that the lobby is cleared out, I am going to join the rest of the team in the conference room. As I walk into the room to take a seat, Agent Murphy stands up and says, "I think we will call it a night. Sergeant Durick, we will be in and out of here tomorrow and will probably meet again as a group the next day. Hopefully by then we will have more information to go on. I will notify all of you with a specific time."

Chapter Twenty-Three - The Woods

She is standing outside my cell door, unlocking it to come in. As she begins to approach me, she reaches into her apron pocket and pulls out a sandwich and a bottle of water and hands them to me. I quickly tear the clear plastic wrap from the sandwich, take a bite, and then gulp down the water. I am getting very thin from only receiving small portions of food, and I am becoming much weaker as each day passes by.

He must be sleeping after his long trip, and that is why she is able to sneak me something to eat. I know she is doing all that she can possibly do to help me without getting caught. Without her I would have starved to death by now.

She is wearing one of her old dresses, and this I can't begin to understand. The front part of this building is beautiful, clean, and furnished with expensive décor. Surely he could afford to buy her some decent clothes. Why does he keep her dressed in rags?

She is sitting next to me on my bed, staring at me as I take each bite of my sandwich.

Reaching over, she gently raises my right hand and places it on her chest. I can feel the necklace that I gave her through the fabric of her dress.

"Thank you for bringing me food. I am glad you like the necklace and that you are wearing it. My dad gave me this locket before he passed away."

Tears start streaming down her face, and she suddenly seems very angry and frustrated. She pushes herself up from the bed and walks toward the door. After stepping into the hallway, she turns back around to lock the door and stares at me with a horrified look on her face.

God, if I could only get inside her mind and know what she is thinking and feeling I could then possibly understand how to reach out to her. When I mentioned my dad, it immediately upset her.

The gown that she gave me is tucked under my mattress. I think she placed it there knowing that if I could eventually get out of this building to get help, I would not want my naked body exposed to the world.

Lying back down on the bed, I begin to think about what he said to me this morning. He is mad at me because I laughed at him, and I know that he is going to be unmercifully cruel to me because of it.

"God, please hear my prayers. I am not afraid to die and join you in heaven, but I am afraid of him and the demons that are living inside of his mind. He deeply resents that I believe in you and that I have so much faith in you as my creator. If you can't help me escape from his demonic ways, please help all of these other women, including the woman who roams the halls. I don't think he was able to abduct another woman on this last trip away from the building, and I fear that he is going to take his sexual sickness out on me again. I ask that you be with me and help me to stay strong enough to survive his brutal ways. Amen."

An hour or so has passed by, and I can hear footsteps in the hallway. He is screaming out my name, his voice getting much louder as he nears my cell.

"Shelby, Shelby, oh Miss Shelby I am coming to get you!"

Looking up, I can see him standing outside my cell door staring in at me. The mask that covers his face is causing me to have flashbacks and feel physically sick. I am

153

sweating, and my heart is racing. His surgical gloves cover his hands as he reaches up with one hand to unlock the door. Quickly walking toward me, he places a saw down on the bed and pulls a rope out of his pocket. He wraps the rope tightly around my wrists and pulls me to my feet. Oh dear God, what is he going to do with this saw? Is he going to cut my fingertips off like he did to Maggie?

He begins to pull me through many different hallways, making several turns. Finally he is stopping by an exit door where he reaches up to grab a shovel. After unlocking the door, we step outside, and I see that we are standing in a dense area of trees and shrubs. Is he going to cut my fingers off and then bury me alive? "Please, God, forgive me for my sins!"

He is pulling me through the timber area, and my feet are being cut up from broken branches and debris lying all over the damp ground. There are a lot of bugs flying in the air, and I can see and smell the mold that is covering some of the trees. This is the same area that he chased me through, and now I will probably be buried here!

I see a truck very close ahead, the same truck that he used to bring me here. As we are getting closer to the truck he is knocking down tall weeds in order for us to get through. He stops, and as I look down I see the body of a very young girl lying a few feet away from the truck. He did abduct another young girl! Her body is naked, but I see no bruising or open cuts on her. Her skin is a pale blue color, and one of her eyes is wide open. My body is shaking all over, and I begin to sob and scream.

"What kind of a mentally sick, perverted beast are you?"

He lays the saw on the ground and begins untying my wrists.

"Start digging, Shelby. Here is the shovel. You have done this before, and you can do it again. The only difference is that this time she is already dead!"

I struggle to dig a hole. The ground is damp, but very hard, and I am so weak. I can't stop crying and shaking. Nobody should have to go through what he has put me and many other women through. Why hasn't he been caught? How can he and so many other evil people go through life without ever having to endure the pain that he has inflicted upon all of us?

I'm sure that I have been digging for at least three hours. My hands are blistered, and I have bug bites all over my body. I don't know how much longer I can do this.

"That should be deep enough."

He is reaching down to pull me out of the hole. I can feel my body sway, and I feel like I could easily pass out. Now he is holding out the saw to me.

"I want you to saw off four of her fingertips for me."

"I can't do that!"

"Do it now, or I will bury you alive with her!"

I have fallen, crying and screaming, next to her body, and I feel as though I am completely shutting down. He is picking up my hand and placing it on top of hers. It is as cold as ice and stiff with rigor mortis.

"I can't do this!"

He is placing the saw in my hand and putting his gloved hand tightly over the top of mine. With his other hand he bends her fingers out and positions the saw over them. He firmly grips my hand, pushes it down, and begins to move it back and forth, back and forth, until her fingertips are severed off. Reaching over with his gloved hand, he picks them up off the ground as though they are just pebbles and places them in his shirt pocket then grabs me firmly by my arm, dragging me onto my feet.

"Start walking toward my truck. Her purse is in there, and it needs to be buried with her!"

At the truck he grabs her purse and hands it to me to carry back to where her body is lying. Shoving her body with his foot, he rolls her into the hole.

"Shelby, throw her purse in on top of her!"

He is reaching into his pants pocket and pulling out a stem of small, white, artificial flowers which he throws on top of her.

"Pick up the shovel and start filling in her grave. And do it quickly; I am being eaten alive by these bugs!"

If only that were true.

I have just finished putting the last shovel of dirt on her grave. He again grabs my wrists and ties them tightly. I am completely overwhelmed with disbelief, guilt, and fear. I am going to be sick! As I bend forward to vomit, he kicks me hard from behind, and I fall to the ground.

"Get up you stupid bitch!"

I am too weak to even try to get back up on my feet. He has walked around me and is standing above my head. Reaching down, he grabs my wrists and begins to drag my body through the weeds and timber. He just keeps dragging me until we are out of the timber and back in the building where he stops to lock the door behind us and to prop the shovel and saw up against the wall. Then he grabs me by the wrists again and continues to drag me through the hallways on my stomach until we reach my cell. He unlocks the door and pulls me in. Leaving me on the floor, he walks out and relocks the door behind him.

"Please God, help me. I can't even move!"

Chapter Twenty-Four - Maze of Information

"Good morning, Sergeant Durick. Agent Murphy called about an hour ago from the Bureau in Chicago, and he would like everyone present at this location at ten o'clock this morning for a meeting. I have already notified the individuals that attended the other meetings."

"Thank you Nancy. You're right on top of it as usual."

"Sergeant Durick, off the record of course, do you think the person that committed this crime is still in Indiana?"

"No, Nancy, but he could very easily return. I am going to check the conference room to see if everything is in order for the meeting and then I will be going to my office. Buzz me if you need anything."

"Yes sir."

"Oh, Nancy, would you mind setting up some coffee and water in the conference room?"

"I have already taken care of it, sir."

"Nancy, you certainly deserve a pay raise."

As I poke my head into the conference room to check it out, I can see that Nancy has already been here to straighten it up. Everything looks good. Glancing up from the doorway I can see all of the colored pushpins sticking out of the map. There are so many women unaccounted for.

After walking to my office and taking a seat at my cluttered desk, it is apparent to me that I need to get caught up on some of my work and get it out of the way. It's very easy to fall behind with everything that's been going on here. I can begin by setting these files on the top of my desk so I can just grab them for the meeting.

An hour has passed, and I have put a dent in the backlog that has been accumulating on my desk. I am very curious to hear what Agent Murphy and his team will be reporting to us this morning. A quick look at my watch tells me it's already nine forty five; I need to head to the conference room.

As I am walking into the room and taking my seat, I see that everyone is here except the agents from the BAU. We all begin to visit back and forth for a few minutes until the door opens and they walk in. The agents are all taking a seat as Agent Murphy walks toward the front of the conference room.

In his prominent and clear voice Agent Murphy says, "Good morning everyone. Thank you all for being here. I am happy to be able to report to all of you this morning that a lot has been accomplished in the last several days. In closely studying the Missing Persons Database and a large number of abduction reports and autopsy reports, we were able to determine that many of these cases have a lot of similarities. The forensic psychologists out of the Chicago office and Agent Daniels spent many hours going through paperwork that was electronically sent from various offices across the United States. Agent Daniels, if you could come up front and go over your findings with everyone, I will take a seat."

"Good morning officers and agents. I would like to inform you all that we are looking for a male suspect between the ages of thirty-two and forty-five. He has been abducting women only during the evening hours and has been extremely cautious about doing this out of the perimeters of any cameras. Upon going over many autopsy reports of women who were abducted and then later found dead, we found that there was a fiber-like material present on each of their bodies. It has been determined that this particular fiber is from a heavy rope material that is used to make commercial fish netting. Some of the other MO's are as follows: he has sexually assaulted all of the women and has used safety measures such as condoms and gloves so as not to leave any DNA or fingerprints. All of the deceased women that have been found had been injected with several different types of street drugs which include tranquilizers, date rape drugs, and several others. He has a pattern of taking their pictures with their cell phones, if they had one, while they are strapped to a bed, naked, and leaving their phones and purses at or near the abduction site. He is keeping their drivers licenses, almost like a sports enthusiast that collects memorabilia.

"The timeframe from the abductions up until their bodies were found tells us that he has held them captive anywhere from at least two days all the way up to several months. The autopsy reports show that they all have been found badly dehydrated and deprived of proper food, as well as having severe lacerations over various parts of their bodies and hemorrhaging under the skin from being brutalized. He has

162

also extracted some of their teeth prior to killing them.

"One of his MO's, that took a while to research, is that he leaves a small stem of flowers with their dead bodies, whether in a shallow grave, a field, a timber area, or wherever the deceased woman was found. After carefully going over all of this information, we found that he is abducting these women from one state and disposing their bodies in a different state. The flowers that he is leaving on their bodies represent the state in which he abducted them. In the case of Margaret Lewis, she was abducted from Illinois, but buried in Indiana. There was a stem of purple violets, which happens to be the Illinois state flower, found on top of her in the shallow grave.

"This perpetrator obviously has deep mental issues as well as sexual issues. He is collecting trophy-type items to make himself feel important and in control. He could be a businessman who works a normal job but feels that he has not been given appropriate recognition, or it could be that he has learned to survive on the streets by distributing illegal drugs as well as using them on these innocent victims. This serial killer obviously has a deep hatred for women.

"This picture of Shelby Grey was digitally enlarged, and you can clearly see that there was a dark wooden wall behind her. Unfortunately this does not tell us if he is traveling around with a bed in a truck or if this is in a building where he has her temporarily held against her will. Agent Durick, I think that someone is tapping on the door."

"Excuse me for interrupting your meeting."

"It's fine, Nancy. Come in. What is going on?"

"Well, sir, we just got another report of a missing girl by the name of Ashley Bennet. Here is the paperwork that just came through."

Agent Murphy is walking toward Nancy to get the papers. He takes a minute to read over them and then crosses to the front of the room where Agent Daniels is standing.

"Let's take an hour recess from the meeting for lunch and meet back here at one o'clock. Once again you may discuss among yourselves what we have gone over during this meeting but not with anyone outside of this meeting. I will see you all back here at one o'clock.

"Sergeant Durick, if you are leaving the building for lunch, would you mind picking me up some type of sub sandwich and an iced tea? I am going to stay here and go over this report that Nancy gave to me. This should cover it."

"Sure, but keep your money. Lunch is on me today."

It is now one o'clock and the meeting is resuming. Agent Daniels is standing at the front of the room again and is beginning to speak.

"I would like to inform all of you that we will be going nationwide with a news conference tomorrow night. Agent Bell has been working on and preparing a report over the last several days. We will be sending an alert to all law enforcement agencies across an eight state area asking them to check all empty and abandoned houses and buildings. We will also be asking them to inform all of their local news stations, as well as local papers, in order to warn the public that we are searching for one of the most notorious serial killers on record. Agent Murphy is now going to go over the report that he received prior to our lunch break."

"Thank you, Agent Daniels. Officers and agents, we received a report of another missing girl out of Nickelsville, Virginia. She was a seventeen year old white female, short blonde hair, and blue eyes. Unfortunately, she was not reported missing until today but was last seen two days ago. Agent Wilson will be doing all of the follow-up investigation on her. Our nationwide news release will be broadcast tomorrow evening from the Chicago headquarters building. I will notify Nancy of our next meeting. Until then, we need to be searching empty buildings in this area and continue patrolling parking lots, parks, and any out of the way secluded areas."

Chapter Twenty-Five - A Chance to Escape

I have managed to inch myself across the floor on my stomach, a little at a time, and pull myself up onto the bed. My body is trembling all over, and I am in extreme pain from being dragged through the timber by my wrists. The skin on my body feels like it is on fire from all of the cuts, bug bites, and bruises, and I am struggling to breathe. I am so thirsty!

If I were to be blessed enough to escape from here, I'm not sure that I could actually explain to anyone what I have been through. I don't think there are words that could begin to express the fear I am carrying inside of me or the torturing sense of guilt I feel for burying two women. Will their bodies ever be discovered, or will their loved ones go through hell the rest of their lives wondering what happened to them? I'm sure my mom is sick and not able to sleep or eat because of not knowing if I am being brutalized or if I am even still alive.

As I slightly turn my head, I can see him quietly standing outside my cell door. I did not hear him coming; he just seems to have appeared out of nowhere like a cat sneaking up on a mouse. I can feel his eyes staring at me from behind that demonic mask, and I hear him breathing deeply in and out. I don't know how long he's been standing there, but at least five minutes have passed in complete silence.

"You have only been sexually abused one night and have yet to be tortured. I will be leaving the building and will return in a few days to change all of that."

His voice sounds very strange, and his behavior is totally out of character! He's walking away. "God, I am relieved to know that he is leaving again, but I am also very aware that he will probably pursue abducting another innocent woman. Please don't let this happen! I know that you have stayed beside me, and that is why I have been given enough food and water to survive. I have not been physically tortured as badly as these other women, and I am very thankful, but please, God, put a stop to all of this."

I must have fallen asleep while talking to God. It's pitch black in the hallway now, and another day has come to an end. I hear a scratching noise on the cell door and the sound of it being unlocked. As I turn my head, I can barely see the dark, shadowy figure walking toward me, but I do smell the appalling scent of her dress. As she comes closer I see her reaching into her apron pocket to take out a bottle of water. She is squeezing her fingers around my arm and trying to help me sit up on the edge of the bed, but my body is quivering, I'm sobbing, and I am very weak. She has taken a seat next to me on my bed, and as I try to drink the water she hands me, she touches what little hair I have left on my head. "Please, why won't you help me?"

I can feel her pushing herself up from my bed and walking away. It is very dark, and I can no longer see her, but I also did not hear the door being shut or locked. "Hello, are you still here?"

There is no answer. I feel my pulse racing, and I am scared. I must try to stand up on my feet and hopefully maintain my balance. Putting my hands straight out in front of me, I am slowly walking forward trying to find the door. I feel the bars and now an open doorway. Oh my God, she has left the door open for me! She is going to help! I'm standing here in disbelief, sobbing! I need to turn back around and find my bed so that I can get that blood-stained gown that she hid for me. Taking small steps back, I bump my leg on the side of the bed. Reaching down, I lift up the mattress and frantically feel all over for the gown. Got it! Ouch! Oh God, my arms hurt as I try to pull it around me. I need to stop and breathe in deeply and concentrate on finding my way out of here.

Once again, I'm walking forward slowly to find the open doorway of my cell. I am walking through it now and into the hallway. I can only hope and pray that I find my way to an exit.

Heading first to the left and then feeling my way to the right, I have reached a wall. Sliding my hand across the damp wall, I feel the chipped paint and smell the mold coming from the cement. My body and mind are feeling loneliness, darkness, and the wretchedness of the beast as I feel my way through this hallway. His crazed ways have caused suffering, terror, and death. This satanic man will someday burn in hell!

I have now come to a corner and need to remember which way we turned to get to the exit the day he made me bury that young girl. I think it was to the left. I can now feel a wall to my left, and I am going to keep walking. "Please, God, help me to remember which way we went!"

Maybe I should be trying to find the elevator. She did show me through the front part of the house for a reason. That could be my only way out of here! We went through the house, down two flights of steps, and through the living area to the front door. There was a row of lights around the circular driveway, and that could lead me to the main road.

I don't know if I could tolerate going through that timber area again. He made me bury her there, and that's the same wooded area he chased me through. I am terrified just thinking about it!

I have reached another corner. I am going to turn right and follow the wall until the next turn. My hands are clammy, and I can feel the sweat beading up on my forehead. It is at least comforting to know that I finally have something covering my naked body.

I have once again come to the end of the wall. I can either go to the left or right, but I think turning right will lead me to the elevator. As my hand is gliding over the rough cement, I touch a metal door. "Please God, let this be the elevator." It is! I need to find a way to slide the door open. I am pushing very hard when suddenly I hear a creaking noise and can feel it slide! Stepping forward, I feel the wood under my feet. I have made it to the elevator! I am turning around to slide the door shut, and as I reach to my left my hand hits a button. I push in on it and hear the horrifying grinding and clanking as the elevator begins to rise!

The elevator has stopped, and I'm sliding the door open. I see a dim light at the end of the hallway. My heart feels like it is going to pound out of my chest, and my insides are quivering. I am running as fast as I can through the house to the first staircase, down the steps, and now through the second story to the staircase, and down the steps again and through the living room. I have reached the front door! I turn the knob and open the door. He is standing there with his arm around her! He reaches out with his other hand and grabs me by my throat. They are both laughing. I have been betrayed!

Chapter Twenty-Six - FBI News Report

"Good evening, agents, and thank you for being here for this brief meeting. We will be broadcasting live within about five minutes. I will introduce Agent Bell, and she will be speaking on behalf of the BAU. We are hopeful that this news conference will assist us in gaining information from the public that might help lead us to a suspect."

"Special Agent Murphy, we are on countdown – five, four, three, two, one."

"Good evening ladies and gentlemen. I am Special Agent Robert Murphy from the Behavioral Analysis Unit out of Washington, D.C. Our team has been called in on a case to assist in finding and capturing a suspect who has abducted women from a minimum of eight different states. Agent Trudy Bell, our Public Information Officer, will continue this conference by speaking on behalf of the BAU. Agent Bell you may proceed with your report."

"Ladies and gentlemen, several days ago information regarding the abductions that have taken place over an eight state area was released to all law enforcement agencies in

173

those states. As many as thirty-three women may have been abducted, and some of them are known to have been brutally molested and murdered. There are possibly fifteen to twenty victims that could still be alive and are being held somewhere against their will.

"After going over the National Missing Persons Database carefully, our agents have determined that these disappearances have many similarities. The abductions all took place on the second, ninth, or twenty-ninth of different months over a span of several years. In all of the cases the abductions took place in the evening hours, and the victims were all white females between the ages of seventeen and thirty-two. They may have been stalked for days prior to their disappearance or could have been randomly targeted.

"A team of forensic psychologists from the bureau has worked diligently on a profile of the abductor. They believe he is a tall man in good physical condition between the ages of thirty-three and forty-five. He is injecting drugs that are believed to have been obtained illegally into his victims. The perpetrator has deep sexual and mental problems and is obviously considered to be highly dangerous.

"We are asking that anyone with any information at all to please notify Agent Robert Murphy at the number on the bottom of your screen. It is very important that the public understands that this man will continue to prey on innocent women. He is very cautious and is an expert at what he does. We would advise all women to be accompanied when going out at night until this predator is apprehended. Once again, if you feel you have any information that would be of assistance in this case, please call. Thank you."

After the reporters leave the room I ask everyone to meet in the small conference room at the end of the hallway in order for Agent Wilson to give us a brief update on the Ashley Bennet case. As we enter the room and take our seats at a small table, Agent Wilson walks toward the front of the room.

"Thank you for arranging this briefing, Agent Murphy. Ashley Bennet was only seventeen years old and, unfortunately, did not have the most attentive parents. They were told that she was going to walk to a friend's house and that she would be spending the night there. The next evening, when she had not called her parents or returned home, they called her friend. Her friend said that she hadn't seen her at all.

The parents did not call the police department until the next morning. Ashley's mother said that her daughter has severe asthma attacks, but she didn't seem that concerned about her being gone since she has done this same thing in the past. Nickelsville, Virginia, is a small community, and the local police are doing an investigation and compiling their report. I have asked the police department to keep us updated. Do you have anything to add Agent Murphy?"

"I think we will call it a night and meet again the day after tomorrow in the conference room at headquarters at nine a.m. With assistance from the forensic psychologists, we will be spending all day tomorrow filtering through each abduction case. Everybody try to get some rest."

Chapter Twenty-Seven - The Basement

With his fingers gripped around my jugular vein and the echoing sounds of their wicked laughter, I feel hopeless and completely betrayed. He is dragging me through the house by my throat with her following close behind. Her face is lit up with excitement as though she is a child getting ready to go to a circus or a favorite amusement park.

I am sobbing and shaking. "Mister, you are hurting me! Where are you taking me?"

We have reached the elevator. As we step in, he shoves me hard enough that I fall to the floor. When I look up, she is reaching toward her neck and gently holding out the necklace, showing it to me, as she continues to laugh. He runs his hand up under her dress, touching her and then fondling her breasts. If he is her husband, how could she condone his sexually molesting other women and filming his actions? She was the one who cleansed their bodies for him to sexually abuse!

The elevator has stopped, and he is reaching down to grab me firmly by my arm. His eyes are staring at me from behind his evil mask as he begins to drag me through the hallways. It is dark. My heart is beating hard in my chest, and I am so afraid. She is briskly following behind us and continues to laugh with her mouth wide open, showing her partial tongue.

He is now yanking my body down a flight of dark, decrepit steps. The stagnant smell of mold is becoming much stronger, and my stomach is churning from fear. He is unlatching an old wooden door, and we enter a dark room. She stretches up on her toes to reach an old oil lantern from a nail on the wall and lights it while he tears off the blood-stained gown that was covering my naked body and forces my arms up over my head. Fastening my hands with ropes that hang from the ceiling, he uses a pulley to lift my body up several inches off the ground. My feet are dangling in the air above the muddy basement floor, and my arms feel like they are being pulled out of their sockets.

This room is thick with cobwebs, and there are large rats crawling everywhere. Oh God, he is going to leave me hanging here to die and be eaten to death by these filthy rats! The pain from the weight of my body pulling on my arms is unbearable.

They are both standing in front of me stripping off their clothes, touching each other's bodies, and performing sexual acts on each other. I cannot stand to think that the last thing I see before I die is his satanic mask and these two very sick animals mating.

They are dressing each other slowly and glaring over at me. He reaches forward and pushes my body with his hands, causing me to swing back and forth while she walks over to turn out the oil lamp. It is pitch black in here now, but I can hear their terrifying laughter and the creaking of the old wooden steps as they are leaving the basement.

"Dear God, is this the way my life is supposed to end? I am afraid. I don't want to be alone my last hours on this earth. Please forgive me for any sins I may have committed, and when the time comes please remain by my side."

I can feel pain shooting through my entire body, and I am becoming weaker and weaker. In order for the rats to survive in this dingy basement, I know they will start chewing on my body.

I must have passed out from the pain. As I try to open my eyes, I see a dim light in the room and his mask in front of me. He is holding a large knife in his hand and is reaching up to cut the ropes from my wrists. I fall face first to the floor. He is reaching down and placing his arms under my armpits, pulling me up onto my feet.

"Stand up, Shelby, and throw this dress on – do it now!"

"Mister, I am too weak and sick. I haven't had anything to eat or drink, and I am badly hurt."

He is putting the dress over my head and pulling it down over my body. He places his arm around my waist and begins hauling me up the steps to the main floor.

"Where are you taking me? Why don't you just kill me and get it over with?"

After many painful steps through several hallways, we have reached an exit. He is unlocking the door, and outside in the darkness I can see a dark blue four-wheel-drive vehicle. He leads me to it, and after opening the door, he pushes me up into the passenger seat. Reaching into his pocket, he pulls out a rope and binds my wrists together. I am very weak, and I feel like everything is spinning around in circles. I can feel myself starting to fade in and out.

"Miss Shelby, wake up. I have driven you to your new home. We are in a root cellar that was built in a remote timber area. The door to the root cellar has been covered with brush and leaves for years, and nobody even knows it exists. They will never find us!"

He lights an oil lamp, and as I look up at him I see that there is no mask covering his face, but I know that wicked voice and those eyes. As I begin to look around the room, I can see the mask hanging from a hook on the wall. Next to it is the picture that was hanging in the den – the one that looked like it had blood splattered all over it. There is a computer sitting on a metal cart, and on the shelves of the cart, there are bottles of medicine, syringes, and needles. I am very sick and confused. I don't understand!

"Lift up your head, Shelby; I am going to feed you some cold soup from this can. You see, my brother was going to kill you like the rest, but you are mine, and I couldn't let him do that. Sip the soup, Shelby. You slept the entire trip, and you are very weak and need to eat."

His brother? "Dear God, are there two of them or does this man have split personalities! I have no idea where I am or what is going on. Please let this come to an end."

"Miss Shelby, I have to leave to make a phone call. Do you need me to give you some medicine for the pain?"

He is walking up the cement steps. I can hear him lifting the metal door and setting it back down and locking it. I can hear the branches and brush scratching against the door as he covers it. Oh God, he is gone! If he doesn't return, I will die here and no one will ever find my body!

Chapter Twenty-Eight - An Anonymous Lead

"Durick residence, may I help you?"

"Sergeant Durick, this is Nancy. I hate to bother you on your day off, but Agent Murphy just called and asked me to notify you that he wants to meet here at headquarters this afternoon at one p.m. instead of tomorrow morning at nine. He said he received an anonymous lead on the case late last night after the news conference."

"Thanks Nancy. Have you notified the others?"

"I wanted to call you first, sir, but I will notify the rest of the officers."

"Thanks Nancy. I will see you about noon."

"Good afternoon, Nancy. I am going to the conference room to make sure that it is set up and ready for the meeting. I am running a little late. Have any of the other officers arrived yet?"

"Yes sir, I believe most of them are in the conference room already."

Walking into the room to take a seat at the table, I see that the other officers are talking among themselves. Agents Miller and Greene are present, so it looks like we are just waiting for Agent Murphy and his team. The door is opening, and Agents Bell and Daniels are taking a seat at the table while Agent Murphy walks to the front of the room.

"Thank you officers and agents for accommodating the change I made in the meeting time. I received an anonymous call last night after the news conference from a man who is an avid reader of murder mysteries. He said that he watched the news conference on TV last night and that, afterwards, he realized that all of the MO's that were discussed had many characteristics similar to those of a series of murder mysteries that were written and self-published by an author named Clayton Morris. He felt that the similarities seemed to be more than just a coincidence and should be checked out.

"After running a check on Morris, we found no criminal background, but when his address was entered into the computer, we found that his residence is located in a remote area of Georgia. After further tracking we discovered, through his social security number, that he retired from an electronics company and purchased a piece of property that included a very large, old mental institution and several acres of timber. Agent Wilson boarded a flight out of Chicago late last night to Georgia and is doing a follow-up and will be contacting us later this afternoon.

"I also received another call last night from a police officer in a small town located just a few hours from Nickelsville, Virginia, where Ashley Bennet was abducted. The officer said that he stopped into a restaurant at the edge of town for a cup of coffee late in the evening on the same night that Miss Bennet was abducted. He said there was a small, white moving van with Georgia plates in the restaurant lot. The officer had a short conversation with the driver of the van who claimed that he was moving some furniture for his sister. We went back into Clayton Morris's records and did a vehicle search and found a small moving van, a 1998 former police vehicle, and a 2013 Cadillac all registered in his name.

"Agent Wilson will be assisted by a team from the field office in that area and will be reporting back to us at about four o'clock our time. Until then, a team out of Chicago is also researching information, and several office staff members have been assigned the task of reading several of Morris's murder mysteries. Hopefully, these leads will steer us in the right direction for finding a suspect. Let's take a fifteen minute break to stretch and get something to drink, and we will continue with the meeting after that."

"Agent Murphy, this is Nancy. You have a call on line one."

"Thank you Nancy. Is it Agent Wilson?"

"No, sir. It's a call from the Chicago office."

"This is Agent Murphy. Yes sir, hold on a second. I am going to put you on speaker phone."

"Agent Murphy, this is Agent Brown. We have completed some more research on Clayton Morris and were able to uncover some pretty interesting facts. Morris was fired from his position at the electronics company. His dismissal was for inappropriate actions with a female employee. He verbally showed anger toward her, and it escalated into him shoving her. According to the Human Resource Department, he was discharged from his job. We were also told that Morris had a definite problem taking directions from women that held a higher position than he did.

"The office staff read three of Morris's books, and your anonymous caller was correct about the similarities between the books and the MO's in these cases. We either have an avid reader of his books who is acting out what he has read, or we have a problem with the author himself. There are too many MO's that stand out in his material - one of them being the state flowers found with the deceased victims.

"Also sir, his mother disappeared in June of 1987, and she was never found. According to the records, Morris was her only child. His father was deceased, and the mother had a live-in boyfriend who was reported missing approximately a year later."

"Thank you, Agent Brown, and please thank the rest of your staff for their assistance."

"Excuse me sir, this is Nancy again. Agent Wilson is waiting to speak to you on the other line."

"Agent Murphy speaking. Yes, Agent Wilson, I am going to put you on speaker phone."

"Agent Murphy, with the assistance of the team, we have been tracking information and speaking to people in the community. According to our contact at the local bank, a large amount of money was withdrawn from Clayton Morris's account yesterday. We took a ride past his residence, and it appears that the front section of what used to be a large mental institution has been renovated into a luxurious home. The back portion of the building that we could see from the road is still in its original state. It is very old and decrepit. We then followed what used to be an old country road behind the building. The road connected to a narrow dirt road where we came across an old police vehicle that was parked partially off the road. The vehicle is registered in Clayton Morris's name, but there were no plates on the car. When we looked through the windows of the car, we saw a box of white surgical-type gloves sitting on the front seat. We lifted a fingerprint off the outside door handle on the passenger side and drove back to the facility and had it processed through the system. The print was that of Shelby Grey. With this evidence we had probable cause to obtain a search warrant from the judge, and we are going in with a SWAT team. We have arranged for back-up troopers and ambulance service. I am sure the media will be right on top of this one! We will keep you updated."

Chapter Twenty-Nine - The Beginning of the End

As I lie here strapped to this bed, naked, the pain that I feel in my body, mind, and heart is unbearable. His words, "You are in your new home now" have diminished any hope that I have been trying desperately to hold onto.

"God, please hear my prayer. It was a human error for me to have taken the life you blessed me with for granted. This very mentally sick man who has ruined so many lives should be punished. I can never forgive his demonic ways. Please help these women who are fighting to stay alive, and somehow show his wife, even though she betrayed me, that she has chosen the wrong path. Amen."

I can hear the sound of the metal key as he is opening the padlock on the door. He has returned and is standing at the end of my bed staring at me. His face is not scarred or disfigured with burns, so why did he always have a mask covering his face? He is glaring at me.

"I will need to catheterize you now, Miss Shelby, and then give you a drink of water. When we are finished we are going to watch the news on the computer through my prepaid wireless internet."

He has finished the game he plays with my mind by touching and feeling me and is now pulling the cart with the computer over next to me and is taking a seat. As the news begins, his facial expressions show signs of anticipation and excitement.

The news anchor is reporting that the FBI received an anonymous phone call that led them to suspects in a serial killing case that they have been investigating. They raided a home located in the front portion of an old mental institution in Georgia. The man and woman that were taken into custody are considered to be the suspects in one of the worst cases of serial killings in history. Eighteen women who were in what the FBI quoted as being "torture chambers" have all been transported either by ambulance or helicopter to hospitals for treatment. All of these women were considered to be in serious or critical condition. The names of the victims and suspects have not been released, but pictures of the two people who were apprehended and taken into custody appear at the top of the screen. The reporter says that footage taken at the scene will be shown on the seven a.m. news tomorrow and that they will be covering the FBI news conference that will be held at six p.m. tomorrow evening.

He is looking over at me and begins to laugh in his haunting voice.

"He will never know that I am the one that made that anonymous phone call. He was allowed to be part of the system, had the opportunity to get an education, and reaped the benefit of physically torturing the women after I brought them back to the building. He had no desire to sexually abuse them because he and my sister have had sexual relations with each other since childhood. Look at the picture that is hanging next to my mask. The two circles that are joined represent them, and I am the circle that is separated and standing off alone. The red paint splatters represent the many women who were sexually abused by me and tortured by my brother and sister. He will never rat me out to the Feds, and she can't speak, read, or write. I will continue to remain free to abduct women and satisfy my mental and sexual needs."

He pushes the cart up against the wall and reaches down to grab a syringe and needle. After drawing medication and filling the syringe, he is walking back toward me and jabs the needle into my arm.

"That will help you get some rest. I am leaving and will be back in the morning to watch the news footage on the computer with you."

He has turned off the oil lamp, and I can hear him as he walks up the steps and lifts up the door to leave.

"Dear God, I can't believe or accept what is happening. I am thankful that the other women were found and will have a chance to live, but I'm sure they, like me, had no idea that there were two of them and she was their sister! If Mister would have left me there, I, too, would have been found. I am beginning to feel lightheaded and nauseated. God and Daddy, I love you."

I begin to open my eyes, but I feel weak and drugged. It is dark, but since I am underground I don't know if it is day or night. I will have to lie here in pain and wonder when this horrific nightmare will all come to an end. I feel like I have cried all of my tears and prayed more than most people would in their entire lifetime.

The scratching of branches being pulled across the metal door has started, and I can hear him taking the padlock off the door. There is daylight creeping through as he lifts the door.

He is coming down the steps and walking toward the cart. His hair has been dyed a different color, and because of his beard he looks different than his brother, but they are the same height and build.

"Well, Miss Shelby, are you ready to watch the footage the reporters recorded?"

The news anchor begins, "Good morning, this is Doug Bauer broadcasting from KLBJ. Our station announced last evening that the FBI raided a home located in Georgia and apprehended two suspects in one of the worst serial killing cases known in history. Here is the footage that was filmed at that location last evening."

As the coverage begins, I see agents from the FBI walking out a tall, muscular man with short hair, slightly balding. Behind him, with cuffs restraining her wrists, is the woman who roamed the halls. The agents take them to vehicles while several EMT's remove the victims, on gurneys, from the building. The location site is taped off, and many agents and officers are guarding the premises. A broadcaster says that no questions asked of the FBI were being answered at this time. As the footage ends, the commentator returns. He expresses his shock at the incident then ends his report with a reminder to "Tune in tonight at six for the live report from the FBI."

After turning off the computer and pushing the cart back to the wall, he tells me that he is going to catheterize me again. As he finishes and wipes me with a rag, he once again begins to touch me.

"This is exciting me!"

He steps back and begins to remove his clothes. Oh God, he is going to rape me again! He begins playing with himself and then swings his leg over me and begins thrusting his penis in and out of me while holding onto my breasts. I hate him! I wish he were dead! He laughs as he puts his clothes back on.

"I am leaving again, Miss Shelby, but thanks for the quickie; it helped me to relax a little. I will be back to watch the six o'clock news. I might bring you back something to eat just so I can keep you alive for a while longer."

He is gone now, and even though I thought there were no more tears left in me, I am sobbing. I feel filthy, and I am to the point that I don't really care if I die.

Many hours have passed, and he still has not returned. My back is hurting me, but I can't reposition my body because of the way he has me restrained. I am thirsty, sick, and in so much pain.

I must have fallen asleep again because I did not hear him open and shut the door. When I opened my eyes he was just standing here staring at me again.

"Miss Shelby, open your mouth so I can pour this broth into you. Chicken broth is so healthy for you. That's good, now a little more. OK, just let it flow down your throat. There, do you feel better? Now for a little water. Open your mouth again, and keep swallowing. I am going to pull the computer over and sit by you so we can watch what the big, bad FBI boys have to say."

A gentleman is introducing himself as Agent Wilson.

"Good evening viewers and ladies and gentlemen of the press. We have in our custody as of yesterday two suspects in a serial killing case that has been under investigation. One of these suspects is a man by the name of Clayton Morris, a murder mystery writer who, we believe, was first committing the crimes and then using them as the plots for his books. The other suspect is a woman who has not been identified. Her fingerprints cannot be traced, but her DNA has revealed that she is a family member of the male suspect. It appears that she cannot speak, read, or write. They have been holding eighteen women hostage in the back portion of what used to be a mental institution. These women were held in individual rooms that we can only describe as torture chambers. According to several hospital spokesmen, they were all sexually, mentally, and physically tortured. At this time the victims' names are not being released.

"There was a room discovered in the front living quarters of this facility with a large map of the United States on which small sprigs of flowers were pinned to different areas of eight states. According to one of Mr. Morris's books, these flowers would represent the women who were abducted from one state and buried in a different state. This is all under investigation.

"While being questioned, with a court appointed attorney present, Mr. Morris refused to answer any questions and has only made one comment: 'You will have all of your questions answered through the book that I will be writing while on death row.'

"I will not be answering any questions from the media tonight, but I can say that this will be a very long and complicated case to solve and process through the court system. At this time the victims are being guarded in the hospitals while getting the medical and psychological treatment needed for them to survive. We are attempting to locate the family members of the victims in order to give them information concerning their loved ones."

The computer is off, and he is pushing the cart back to the wall.

"I need something for the pain."

He fills another syringe and walks back toward me. He jabs the needle into my arm and replaces the syringe on the cart then reaches up to grab his mask and place it over his face.

"That quickie with you earlier sparked my need to search out and abduct another woman. I may return or maybe not. Enjoy the drug I administered to you!"

"Dear God, I need to believe you are hearing my prayers. The FBI will remove my necklace from the woman who roams the halls. I know that since I am not one of the victims to have been found alive, they will assume I am dead. Please be with my mother. Give her the strength that she will need, and if he does not return, please let death come quickly for me. He preyed upon me, and now I am praying to you. Amen"

Made in the USA
Charleston, SC
19 February 2015